D1827343

HOLLOW NIGHT

C1066

HOLLOW NIGHT

HOLLOW NIGHT

Cynthia Harrod-Eagles

Chivers Press • **G.K. Hall & Co.**
Bath, Avon, England • Thorndike, Maine USA

This Large Print edition is published by Chivers Press, England, and by G. K. Hall & Co., USA.

Published in 1997 in the U.K. by arrangement with the author.

Published in 1996 in the U.S. by arrangement with Dorian Literary Agency.

U.K. Hardcover ISBN 0–7451–4935–9 (Chivers Large Print)
U.K. Softcover   ISBN 0–7451–4946–4 (Camden Large Print)
U.S. Softcover   ISBN 0–7838–1845–9 (Nightingale Collection Edition)

The text of this Large Print edition is unabridged.
Other aspects of the book may vary from the original edition.

To Anthony, fellow SF groupie, with love

Set in 16 pt. New Times Roman.

Printed in Great Britain on acid-free paper.

British Library Cataloguing in Publication Data available

Library of Congress Cataloging-in-Publication Data

Harrod-Eagles, Cynthia.
  Hollow night / Cynthia Harrod-Eagles.
  p. cm.
  ISBN 0–7838–1845–9 (lg. print : sc)
  1. Large type books. I. Title.
[PR6058.A6945H6   1996]
823′.914—dc20   96–20629

CHAPTER ONE

Bee was in the kitchen straining the vegetables when the door-bell rang, so Paul went to answer it. He was only half way down the hall when Bee overtook him at a run. She actually bounced as she passed him, a funny little jump of sheer excitement, and he stood back and smiled indulgently, letting her beat him to the door. She opened it and Louise and Clifford were there wearing identical grins.

'Come in, come in! You're early,' Bee cried. The two women embraced enthusiastically—they were old friends, had been at college together. Clifford stooped to kiss Bee too, and handed her a bottle of wine still wrapped in its tissue paper.

'Oh Clifford—how kind!' Bee exclaimed, just as if it were not the established custom in their group for dinner guests to bring wine. Paul and Clifford exchanged a tight smile over Bee's head, and when they could get to each other, shook hands with reserved dignity as became their status as husbands of the friends.

'Hullo. How's it going?'

'Oh—you know. How's tricks with you?'

'Same as ever. You're looking well.'

Paul shut the door behind his guests and followed them down the hall. Louise had run on ahead and was poking her head excitedly round each door as she came to it and exclaiming on what she saw.

'But, Bee darling, you've done so much! I simply can't believe it!'

'Oh, not so much really,' Bee said modestly. 'We were very caught up, you see, with painting the outside—'

'But it's so much better than when we were last here!' Louise broke in relentlessly. 'Honestly, I just can't believe it's the same place, it looks so different.'

'It's the same place,' Paul assured her, but she didn't hear.

'Cliff, come and look. Look what they've done with this room.' Without waiting for her husband to reach her at the door she turned to Bee again. 'I love that colour. That colour is absolutely—'

'Paul chose that. I wanted something a little warmer, but now we've got it up I like it. He—'

'It's perfect. It makes the room look so *big*.' There was a moment's silence as she gazed and Paul opened his mouth to offer them a drink but wasn't quick enough. She was off again.

'I must see what you've done in the dining-room,' she said, hastening down the passage. Bee trotted in her wake like a faithful retainer, and the men strolled after them again, talking about brands of paint and the merits of polished floors as against carpets.

They caught each other up again in the garden, where Louise was telling Bee that she had done marvels considering, and Bee was telling Louise that she had actually had three crops off the beans but they were all finished now so you couldn't tell.

'Would anyone like a drink?' Paul asked loudly, recognising that breaks were not going to present themselves.

'I thought you'd never ask,' Clifford smiled, but Bee swung round with an expression of horror and cried,

'My God, I'd forgotten. I was just taking the vegetables off when the bell rang. Excuse me, won't you—I'll have to—' and she hared off down the garden. The other three watched her go, and then turned to stroll more slowly towards the house, whose lighted windows were beginning to glow pleasantly in the gathering dusk.

'It's a nice house,' Clifford said at last, warmly. 'It's got a friendly look about it.'

'I'm glad you like it,' Paul said politely, for he didn't really care if anyone else liked it—his own opinion was enough. But he added with more emphasis, 'It's a *good* house. Built at the right period. The proportions are good. As I tell Bee, proportions are everything.'

'It's practically the same period as ours,' Louise put in.

'No it's not, Lulu,' Clifford contradicted her gently. 'There's about a hundred and fifty years' difference.'

'Oh well,' she swept away the offending

3

century and a half with a wave of her hand. 'It looks a lot like it.'

'The layout's similar,' Paul conceded generously.

'Identical.' Louise wanted a point.

'Apart from our funny kitchen.' Paul gave her half a point.'

'Oh yes—the kitchen. I must see what you've done there.'

'Not now. I think we'd better go and sit down, or Bee will have kittens.'

An unfortunate expression as it turned out, for it triggered off connections in Louise's grasshopper brain.

'How *is* Bee?' she asked earnestly. Paul did not answer for a moment, but involuntarily his footsteps slowed and his brows drew slightly together. Seeing this Clifford touched his wife's arm reproachfully, but she shook off the touch like a verbal reproof.

'Oh, she's taking it very well,' Paul said quietly, 'but one can't help knowing she's still very cut up inside.'

'That's only natural,' Clifford said gently. 'It takes a long time to get over something like that. After all, it's only a few months, isn't it?'

'Nearly a year, actually.'

'Is it that long? Time does fly, doesn't it,' Clifford said.

'It was August the thirteenth. It was a Sunday,' Paul said dully. 'I'll never forget it.'

Now Louise turned a reproachful eye on

4

Clifford in her turn. 'You don't get over losing a baby that quickly,' she said, as if it were Clifford's fault.

'It'll be a year next week,' Paul said. 'I'm dreading the day coming round. She can't help but be reminded.'

'What will you do? Take her out somewhere?'

'I don't think so. That would be rather—obvious, wouldn't it?'

'Perhaps if we invited you both over—?'

'Thanks, Cliff. That's kind of you. Perhaps if you could do it without—sort of making a point of it, or mentioning the date—'

'Soul of tact,' he said, smiling professionally. 'I'll slip it in so she won't even notice she's saying yes.'

They reached the house and by tacit consent dropped the subject.

'Are you all there?' Bee's voice came from the kitchen. 'Will you all sit down, and I'll dish up. It's all ready.'

As they stepped over the threshold Clifford became aware of a throbbing sound—actually hardly a sound, more like a distant vibration; it was the sort of sound that might be made by a heavy lorry running its engine outside in the street. He paused at the garden door, holding his head back so that it was outside the house, listening.

'What's up?' Paul asked, turning back to catch him in his strange attitude. The noise had

5

stopped. A lorry, probably. Or even a plane, very high up.

'Nothing. Do you get much aircraft noise here?' Clifford asked.

'Oddly enough, only on fine days. We are in a flight path, but they only use it when the wind's in a certain direction, and that's the direction that brings sunny weather. When it's cold and rainy and no-one would want to sit out in the garden, you never hear or see a 'plane at all.'

Clifford smiled dutifully and followed his host into the dining-room. Louise hung back to call down the passage to the kitchen.

'Can I help, Bee?' There was no answer, and she cocked her head to catch any indicative sound. 'Bee?'

'Yes?' the voice came back after an appreciable pause, sounding far off.

'Can I give you a hand?'

Another pause. 'No, I'm just coming. Sit down. Paul can pour out some wine.'

Louise and Clifford exchanged glances. They both wondered if she'd been crying, and Clifford wondered additionally if she'd overheard anything of what they'd been saying. In a moment, however, she appeared in the doorway holding a dish with a cloth, and smiling, her eyes innocent of moisture.

'What a job it is to get you lot to sit down,' she said cheerfully.

After the lull of the first few mouthfuls,

6

Louise cast around in her mind for a neutral topic of conversation.

'How's your cat?' she asked at last. 'He generally comes out to meet us—I haven't seen him tonight.'

Bee didn't look up.

'Oh, Footsa? Didn't I tell you—he ran away.'

'Oh.' Louise was taken aback. 'I'm sorry. What a shame.'

'Poor little soul,' Bee went on, 'I think he must have gone away to die. He'd been very ill, and then one day he just disappeared. We had a cat once before that did that—do you remember, Paul, old Joxer?—he got lower and lower and then went off by himself and never came back.'

Curse, Louise was thinking, is there no safe subject? Clifford, with a better understanding, took up the subject.

'What was wrong with Footsa, then? Did you take him to the vet?'

'No, I didn't—you see, there was nothing really you could put your finger on. He just seemed mopey, and then he went off his food. He slunk about with his head down and flinched when you tried to touch him. And then one day—just wasn't there.'

'Maybe it was just old age,' Clifford said.

'That's what I told her,' Paul said.

'He wasn't all that old,' Bee said. 'He was only ten.'

'Maybe he'd had a hard life,' Clifford said, giving Bee a wink with the side of his face away from Louise. Louise looked up at him, shocked, and then saw Bee smiling. Sympathy flooded her.

'Poor, Bee, you have had a hard time, haven't you?'

Bee's smile froze over, and both Clifford and Paul looked down hastily at their plates in the embarrassment of the moment. Bee's eyes filled with tears and for a second Louise thought she really would break down; hoped she would, for then at last she would be able to get out of her what she really felt about it all—losing the baby and being told she could never have another. Bee had always been the one who wanted children—she had been quite sure about it, even in their undergraduate days; it had been one of her firm ambitions, at a time when the rest of them didn't even know what they thought about the opposite sex.

For Bee to be the one to be stricken with barrenness seemed to all of them an unnecessarily ironic twist of fate; yet Bee seemed to have accepted it quietly and fatalistically, at least with her public face. Paul said she felt badly about it, and of course one naturally assumed she did, but she never gave any indication. Even now the tears seemed to go back whence they had come so quickly that one almost doubted they had been there at all.

'Oh, no worse than other people,' Bee said

8

cheerfully. 'You have to expect a little heartbreak when you have pets.'

Well, that seemed a fairly distinct 'keep off' notice. Louise nodded coolly and went on with her soup. She longed for Bee to make a confidante of her, but she had got to the stage where she didn't really expect it ever to happen. Bee had always been the mature one of the group, and it was to her they had all taken their young problems for her advice and guidance. Of course, they rarely took her advice—they rarely, as a species, took anyone's advice, those bright young things of the sixties—but the fact remained that she was the one they felt they could talk to. She was never shocked by anything, and though she never actually told you anything about her own life, you got the feeling that she had done everything you'd done long before you'd ever thought about it, and lots more besides. She gave the impression of having come up the hard way. It was even rumoured that she had had an affair with one of the lecturers.

The dinner went on its way, and the wine blunted the edges of everyone's feelings so that topics of conversation naturally arose and remained neutral. Since all four of them were in the throes of doing up their first house, the conversation naturally returned again to plaster and paint and knocking down walls.

'We still haven't seen what you've done with your kitchen,' Louise said suddenly.

9

'Oh, yes, you must come and see that. As soon as you've finished,' Bee said enthusiastically.

'We've had to be very careful,' Paul took it up, 'because, believe it or not, bits of that wall are actually protected. It's very, very old.'

'We knew it was old, but not that old,' Clifford laughed. 'I didn't think they slapped orders on people's sculleries.'

'Well, you can see it doesn't belong to the house,' Paul said. 'It seems from what the man from the DOE said that there was originally another house on the site of this one, and that the present kitchen was part of *that* house—the chapel, in fact. Then the house got knocked down, leaving the kitchen intact, and this house was eventually built on the site.'

'Why on earth did they knock down the house and leave the kitchen?' Louise asked.

'Search me,' Paul shrugged. 'It looks jolly rocky, but in fact it's got very deep foundations. Maybe the rest of the house just fell down, leaving that bit. But anyway, there it is. I'd as soon tear it down completely and start again, but—'

'Vandal!' Bee cried. 'You leave my kitchen alone. I love it. It gives me a lovely feeling to think it's so old. And you should just see what we've found under the floor—!'

'Sh! Don't spoil the surprise,' Paul stopped her.

'Under the floor?' Louise asked, puzzled.

'Yes, all that tatty old concrete—you remember,' Bee said. 'We dug it all up to replace it—it was all broken and cracked and crumbling.'

'I remember—it was,' Clifford nodded. 'What did you get it up with?'

'A pick,' Paul grimaced. 'I can still feel the blisters. But once we saw what was underneath we went at it with a chisel, very carefully. And it was worth it, believe me.'

'Oh come on!' Louise cried impatiently, pushing her chair back. 'Stop tantalising us. Let us see. Is it treasure? You know you can't keep it if it is.'

'It's treasure all right,' Paul said, 'but we haven't reported it yet. Frankly, I don't know that we will.'

'No,' Bee said sharply. 'You report it and they'll come and take it away. Don't say anything to anyone. Leave it alone.' She stood up as she spoke, and they turned to look at her, surprised at the vehemence of her tone. But they put it down to general strangeness when she said, 'You two must promise not to tell anyone. Promise!'

'All right,' Clifford said quickly, to soothe her. 'But we don't know what we've promised not to tell anyone about. For heaven's sake show us this mysterious find, before we blip you on the head.'

Bee's taut face relaxed into a smile and she jumped up from her place in her usual gay

11

manner. 'Come on then!'

The kitchen was down a short passage from the dining-room, past the back door, for it stood out beyond the house and was, in fact, as Paul had explained, not really a part of it structurally. At the end of the passage there was one step down and as they reached the step they could see what they had been brought to see, for there was no door to the kitchen, just an open doorway.

It was a square stone structure, the stone white-washed without being plastered and it was roughly furnished with the makeshift kitchen items they had bought to tide them over until the structural work was done. But the floor had been cleared, and where, on their last visit, the guests had seen decaying concrete, they now saw an almost flawless marble mosaic made up of small pieces of green and white stone.

'My God,' Clifford breathed in awe.

'It's beautiful,' Louise cried out, and was about to step down onto it when Clifford caught her by the arm and kept her still where she was, standing above it in the doorway.

'It's called a maze—the pattern, I mean,' Paul said. 'There are lots of other examples all over the country, some in mosaic like this, but mostly done with white paths on green turf in peoples' gardens and so on. It's apparently an ancient, traditional design. Like those square keys the Greeks used.'

'It's not really a maze,' Clifford said. 'Not like Hampton Court maze, I mean.'

'No, not like that. But it is a continuous path—if you imagine the white bit is the path and the green bits the dividing hedges, you can follow the path from the bottom—*there*—into the middle and out again. One long, continuous path.'

They stared at the white pattern on its green background, tracing the line with their eyes. Louise said impatiently, 'It doesn't look like a maze to me. It looks like a brain. You know, those diagrams of the human brain you see in medical text-books.'

Bee glanced at her sharply. 'You see that too, do you?'

'Kind of mushroom shaped,' Louise elaborated. 'Why, did you see it that way?'

'It occurred to me.' She stared at it again. 'Marvellous, isn't it?'

'Tremendous,' Clifford said vigorously. 'And in such perfect condition.'

'Yes, that's the funny thing about it,' Paul said. 'When we came to chip the concrete off, it came quite easily, in big chunks, without touching the marble at all. And do you know what we found?'

'What?'

'Whoever had concreted it over, had *greased* it first—so it wouldn't be damaged.'

'Well, that was nice of them,' Louise said. 'Very thoughtful.'

'But,' Clifford said, bewildered, 'If they thought so much of it, why did they cover it up in the first place?'

'That's what I wondered,' Bee said musingly.

'Perhaps they were just fed up with it,' Louise put in. 'I suppose it isn't everyone's taste.' She stepped down onto the kitchen floor, and at once shivered convulsively.

'Cold?' Bee asked her solicitously.

'A goose walked over my grave,' she said automatically.

'I'll get you a cardigan if you like.'

'No, I'm not cold. It was just the change in atmosphere I expect.'

'Your arms have gone all goosey,' Bee said. Clifford, standing behind her, looked at the pimpled skin on the backs of her upper arms.

'Funny,' he said, 'what primitive reactions we still harbour. You feel cold, so your skin tries to make your non-existent fur stand up to trap the warm air under it.'

'I'm not cold,' Louise said irritably. She rubbed her arms and the goose pimples subsided. 'Well, it certainly is a find, but what are you going to do with it?'

'Do? I don't know.' Bee stared at the pattern. 'It could be of any age. But I don't want archaeologists trotting in here and claiming it for the nation.'

'Well, what will you do then? Cover it up again?'

14

'Cover it up!' Paul exclaimed with simulated horror. 'You're like the vandals who lived here before us! Of course we won't cover it up—we've only just uncovered it.'

'But it'll be awfully cold and hard,' Louise said uncertainly. 'Imagine walking about on that all day long. It'll make your legs swell up.'

'Never mind Lulu darling,' Bee laughed affectionately, putting her arm round her friend's shoulder. 'It'll be easy to keep clean. And after all, lots of people are going in for quarry tiles nowadays, and spending fortunes getting floors not a tenth as lovely as this one.'

'Quarry tiles don't have little cracks in them like this mosaic,' Louise insisted gloomily. 'Most unhygienic in a kitchen.'

'I don't expect it was originally designed for hygiene,' Bee said equably. 'How about some coffee? If you've all admired my floor sufficiently you could go and sit in the drawing-room, and I'll bring it through.'

'Good idea, Bee—I'll put the kettle on,' Paul said, eager to break up what might turn into an argument.

'No, it's all right, I'll do it,' Bee said, crossing the kitchen to the sink, where she filled the kettle and then carried it across to the gas stove. Clifford noticed that on both journeys she stepped carefully round the white pattern in the centre of the floor.

CHAPTER TWO

They were all sitting round the empty hearth in the drawing-room when Bee called from the kitchen,

'Can someone carry some cups, please?'

Paul and Louise, who were arguing about the relative pleasures and troubles of being self-employed, both moved to get up, but Clifford was on his feet before them and said, 'I'll go,' so firmly that they subsided into their chairs again without even noticing that they had moved. He walked down the dim passage from the brightly lit room towards the other bright patch of the kitchen, and their animated voices followed him comfortingly, absorbed in their argument.

Bee was standing at the table to one side of the door, hidden until you reached the doorway. She turned her head at the sound of his footsteps, and he stepped down onto the green marble, in the lee of the doorway, and took her gratefully in his arms. He was over a foot taller than her, and even though he stooped to her she still had to stand on tiptoe to reach him. They were still for a long time, her hands on his shoulders, his round her waist, their faces together, his tongue deep in her mouth, its tip pressed against the muscular tip of hers as she swallowed his saliva that ran

16

down it.

Then at the same moment, as if by prearrangement, they stepped back from each other, and Bee wiped her mouth nervously on the back of her hand.

'Strange how people always have to touch their faces when they're nervous,' Clifford said lightly, to disguise his feelings.

'You're full of physiological titbits tonight,' Bee retorted. 'Perhaps you'd like to explain the phenomenon of tumescence?' They both looked down at the tell-tale hump in his trousers, and as he laughed softly she flung herself against him and hugged him hard, in earnest this time, her face pressed to his chest which was as far up as it reached when they were both on flat feet. He edged his hips forwards to get the relief of pressing against her, and she returned the pressure, gripping his buttocks and pulling him forward fiercely; her next words were muffled.

'What?' he asked, and he pushed her from him gently and wearily, knowing this did not help.

'I said Oh God, actually,' Bee answered, sounding quite calm. 'Why can't we do anything about this? Why are we so tight with bloody social restrictions? Animals don't have this problem.'

'On the other hand, animals don't feel either love or desire, just rut.'

'Which do you feel?'

'Both. All three I suppose. I want to have you, right now, and here, but I also love you and want to have you tomorrow, and everywhere.'

'What pretty things you say,' Bee said listlessly.

'It's your choice,' he reminded her. 'It always has been.'

'Not my *choice*,' she answered wryly. 'I don't choose. My God, do you think I would have chosen—' She was silent. He put out a hand and touched her hair where the fine ends made a nimbus round her head. Her eyes filled quickly with tears as they met his. 'Oh don't,' she breathed. 'You break my heart.'

'Bee—'

'We'd better take in the coffee before they send a search party.'

Wildly he thought of grabbing her hand and running away with her that very instant, but even while one part of his brain was thinking it the other half was making him pick up the tray of cups she had put out ready. 'I'm more civilised than I knew,' he said aloud. Bee made no comment. She went to the stove for the coffee-pot and again he noticed that she did not tread on the pattern on the floor.

'The time will come,' she said. He stood back and let her pass ahead of him.

'Will it?'

'Oh yes.' She walked on a few steps, and then said, without looking at him, 'Actually I sound

18

more confident than I am. And *that's* civilisation too.'

* * *

Later that night Paul lay in bed watching Bee undress. He was always in bed before her because by a tradition that had grown up around them without design on either part, she performed the rituals of switching off and locking up. The last thing she did was to tidy the bedroom, and she moved around now folding things and putting things away, lit from one side by the bedside lamp like a dancer in the finale of *Swan Lake*.

He always thought she moved like a dancer still; in slow motion it was a graceful movement, each foot feeling for the floor in a tentative, stretching way, her body following after like water flowing down an incline. When she moved fast it became ungainly, so that she appeared always to be on the point of falling over, her limbs flying away from her hurrying body like a new foal's. Now, last thing at night, moving softly in the half-dark and drawing the clothes from her body, it was at its most beautiful.

'You looked lovely tonight,' he said. She looked up in surprise, as she always did when he complimented her, as if she were afraid it was the opening move in a gambit to disadvantage her.

19

'Did I? Thank you.'

'Yes, you did. Don't look so surprised. You *are* beautiful, you know.' He settled his hands under his head to watch in comfort, feeling rather like a sultan having his prized possessions displayed before him for choosing. She caught the hem of her dress with crossed hands and drew it up and over her head, and it clung silkily as she pulled it away from her body as if, warm and smelling of her as it was, it was unwilling to be parted from her. She had gained a fine tan that summer and it made her skin shine like polished metal. She was like a little bronze dancer from feet to neck; but the curls around her head were as soft as a child's.

She passed her hands behind her now to unhook her bra, and it dragged forward with the weight of her released breasts. She put down the garment and ran her hands under the fullness, rolling the breasts luxuriously in her palms; then stooped and quickly jerked off her pants. The flesh was pure, pearl white where her bikini had been; it gleamed against the dark shine of her tanned skin as if it had been specially marked out for his attention— provocative, erotic. Start here, it said, and go on to there. He felt himself grow, his penis stretching itself painfully like someone who has fallen asleep in an awkward position. He put his hand to it under the sheet much as she had rolled her hands under her breasts to ease them after long confinement.

She climbed into the bed naked—neither of them ever wore nightclothes—and reached out to switch off the light.

'No,' he said. She stopped and looked at him apprehensively. 'I want to look at you.'

He made no move, so she lay down, on her back, as she slept, and remained still, staring at the ceiling. When she had relaxed a little he reached out and pulled off the sheet, drawing it back slowly to reveal her inch by inch. It was like unveiling a new statue, a bronze nymph, except that her white breasts were now very definitely not of metal. They were soft, and slipped sideways under their own weight. In the centre of each, a dark-rose nipple stood up starkly from its surrounding silken skin, glaring at him rigidly, defiantly hard in her softness.

He could see now how, despite the pads of fatty flesh here and there, she was thin. Her rib cage stood out like that of a starving cow; he could count the ribs even on her upper chest, and her shoulders looked sharp enough to spike himself on. All her bones seemed to point forward: the top of her sternum, her hip bones, and bony arch of her pubis, all leaned forward as if to draw attention to themselves. When she lay flat on her back her spine did not touch the bed. From buttocks to shoulders her body curved like a bridge over a stream.

He slid his hand under the forward-arching pubis and let his fingers reach into the warm

21

moistness, and as he did so she closed her eyes and he knew she had gone into hiding again. She relaxed her legs obediently so that, like handling a corpse, he could part them and work his way in. Once in he could not stop himself. She held onto him, hands firmly on his buttocks, an impersonal firmness like that of a trainer; she worked with him, gripping him inside and moving to him, the other half of each thrust and withdrawal; as he neared climax she made little soft, sad noises, whimpering as if he were hurting her and she were too weak to pull away—noises that excited him unbearably; but all the time her eyes remained closed, she would never look at him, and he could never be sure she was actually there.

This time she came with him, crying out loud like real pain and arching so strongly upwards that she lifted him and his knees came off the bed. His convulsions were so strong that if felt as if his body would turn itself inside out; he felt emptied out, a hollow shell. For a time he drifted away, lying flat across her as spent as a dead firework; and then he was called relentlessly back to consciousness by the knowledge that she was crying.

She did it very circumspectly. She scarcely moved, and made no sound, but he could feel how rigid her body was, lifting slightly off the bed with its tension, and the tears that flowed silently out of her eyes were wetting his face.

Sometimes she cried in the middle of the night, and he would wake from dreams of burst pipes or rainstorms to find the pillow soaked and her tense body practically levitating in her effort not to move as she cried. At those times he would roll over against her and groan as if in his sleep, and the distraction was sometimes enough to stop her crying. He never let her know he had woken, feeling that if she went to such lengths not to wake him, it would be additional cruelty to her to let her know he had been disturbed.

It was different now, though. Had no-one ever told her that to cry when you had just been made love to was the worst thing you could do to a man's ego? He rolled off her, and then gathered her into him like a child, and to his surprise and, unexpectedly, relief she let go at once and sobbed aloud and convulsively, real, ugly crying like somebody transported with grief.

'What's the matter? Why are you crying?' he asked. She couldn't answer of course, but he was so distressed he continued to ask her in the intervals of stroking her head and saying ineffectually, 'There there. Ssh. It's all right.' Why does one say these things? Stupid, stupid. One even starts on 'Don't cry,' given long enough, and that surely is the most stupid.

Gradually she slowed and calmed. 'Bee,' he said. 'Bee. Darling, why do you cry? Why do I make you cry?'

She said something incoherently through her subsiding sobs. She tried again and it came as 'Not you. Not make me. Not your fault.' She didn't want to say any more, he could tell, and he held her in silence until she had stopped, and was shaken only by the occasional shudder. She sat up and reached unglamorously for a handkerchief and blew her nose loudly and wetly. Her face was swollen so that her eyes were only pink puffed slits with the wet spiky lashes sticking out at right angles. She looked like a burn victim with all the pink, tight, shiny skin. Crying is not elegant. After a minute she switched off the light and lay down again, flat on her back. In the dark he could hear her jerky breathing gradually regularising.

Leave well alone, said his better sense. He knew why she cried, but wouldn't admit it to himself. What instinct of suicide made him want to hear her say it, and make it undeniable? He rehearsed the words in his head so often that he almost fell asleep. He woke to full consciousness with a jerk, knowing by her breathing that she was still wakeful. He knew why she went rigid when he touched her sexually, why she arched under him so that her body was a hollow skeleton into which he would climb without touching the sides, why the sexual act made her weep. Why ask her? He knew.

'Why did you cry?' He heard his voice with a

sense of fatality. Her voice came back through the dark with no trace of crying, very calm, very factual, like the voice of God that saints are supposed to hear in the night to call them to their vocation.

'Because I am barren. It makes the whole thing seem so futile, when I know it can't lead to anything.'

He fell asleep instantly. Bee continued to stare at the ceiling in the dark for some time, and then she turned into her side with her back to Paul and fell asleep too.

*   *   *

Paul woke some unknown time later and lay wondering what had woken him. Turning his head he could just make out the clock face, and after staring at it for some time he decided it was half past two: the hands were not luminous. He turned his head the other way and saw Bee was not there—that must be what woke him—Bee getting up. She often went to the bathroom in the night. He turned over luxuriously on his side, and then it started again—a heavy, muted vibration. As soon as heard it he remembered waking to it. A jumbo going over, he thought. The take-off roar is heavier and more vibrating than the landing roar. He settled more deeply into his pillow, and wondered if it was his imagination or if the bed shook silently.

Half past two? He must have read the clock wrong. Planes don't take off at that time of night. Do they? He thought not—government regulations, not to wake up the good sleeping citizens. Ha! Well it had stopped now anyway. Bye bye, plane. Off to Istanbul or Greece or Salisbury. Daft. Much better be in bed, warm. He snuggled down. Bee drifted in ghostlily and got quietly into bed beside him.

'Where've you been?' he asked sleepily.

'For a drink of water,' she said. She jerked over onto her side and they slept, and the house was silent.

*   *   *

Bee and Clifford met the next day outside the British Museum. Bee was a little early and Clifford a little late so between them she had about ten minutes to wait. The entrance, gates and steps where as a student she had sat in worship were thick with Middle-Eastern and French tourists, some of whom seemed to be camping there. There were three hot-dog/hamburger stalls outside the gates and the pavements were stained with grease and littered with screwed-up papers, while the air was redolent with tomato sauce, mustard and vinegar. The man at the stall nearest to Bee was filthy and while there were no customers picked his nose busily and with professional thoroughness. Bee began to feel very queasy.

26

She studied the opening times of the British Library earnestly and then began to count the number of 'e's in the notice—anything to keep her mind occupied and away from painful things.

'Sorry I'm late—Bee?'

She turned eagerly and felt her heart give a giant, schoolgirlish lurch at the sight of him.

'Quick, let's get out of here—I can't stand the smell,' she said. They began to walk very fast down the road, close together but not touching. They walked down Coptic Street and crossed New Oxford Street into Shaftesbury Avenue. Bee said, 'Lunch first? How long have you got?'

'Certainly lunch first,' Clifford said. 'That'll make it last longer.'

Bee snorted with laughter. 'You sound like a bloke I had once. He used to do breathing exercises to stop himself coming. I used to lie there trying not to laugh while he counted up to five over and over again, and recited rhymes.' They had paused at the traffic lights and Clifford took her elbow and stared down at her, offended. She saw his pupils contract and his nostrils flare suddenly, and felt her own answering flutter of desire, like a thump right in the opening of the vagina.

'Right,' he said sternly, 'That's it. I'm not going to be compared with someone who made you laugh. We'll go straight there and then we'll see who's laughing.'

27

'Ooh, you are masterful,' she said coyly, and as the lights changed he grabbed her arm firmly and held it up so that she walked with a list like a dog pulling at its lead; he trotted her across the junction and down Monmouth Street where they had a bedsitter over a shop. They paid half the rent each so that neither felt tied to the other by financial bonds, and each had a key.

They let themselves in with Bee's key and ran quickly up the stairs and inside, shutting the door with something like panic, as if they were afraid they would be caught before they had gone to earth. The room contained a bed, a chair, a sink, and a gas ring on a rickety table. Bee had lived in worse, but to Clifford it was a novelty, like anything miniature that actually works: he had always been well off.

As soon as they were inside Bee flung herself at him and pressed her body to his, feeling his penis already rocklike against her. Clifford bent his head to her she pushed her tongue into his mouth urgently, and with their faces stuck together he put his hands under her skirt and straight to the wet, ready opening. He pulled her panties away and made to kneel down and kiss her there, but she plucked anxiously at his shoulders and said.

'No, please just do it, now. I want you in me right now. We can do all that later—just one quick one, for me.'

His eyes held hers like a lepidopterist's hot

28

pins, and she backed to the bed with her firm dancer's steps, and standing on one foot at a time neatly hooked off her pants. It was hot, and she was wearing nothing but pants and a cotton dress but she had no time to remove the latter. He struggled with his zip, dropped trousers and pants to half mast, and was onto the bed and in her in the same movement.

She came almost instantly, breaking into a series of sharp jerks like a threepenny jumping-jack, and he came seconds later. It was so quick they were not even out of breath.

'Now I know why they call it banging,' she said, stroking his hair in kindness.

'Is that all?' he whined. 'I wouldn't of paid first if I'd known that was all it was going to be.'

'Never mind son, you'll know better next time. Next time cross your legs and count up to ten.'

He kissed her tenderly on the lips, and then on either eye. 'Darling,' he said, and then, 'You've been crying again?'

'Oh God, does it show that much?'

'Only to the eyes of love. Your eyelids are shiny.'

'Can't get away with a thing. Not today, though—last night.'

'Oh. Did he—' Clifford began to draw away, and his voice had taken on an edge of coldness.

'It wasn't his fault,' she said, pretending to misunderstand him. 'I just cried anyway. I
29

often do.'

'I know *that*,' he said, trying not to sound relieved. 'How are things with you anyway? You seemed all right together yesterday.'

'He's always at his best in front of guests. Anyway, Cliff, he doesn't abuse me or anything—now. He just doesn't love me.'

'Oh come—of course he does. He's said so.'

'Not to me.'

'No? Well, he's said so to Lulu, and why should he lie to her?'

'To impress her, maybe,' Bee said listlessly. 'Anyway, why are we discussing him again? I never seem to be able to get away from him.'

'Well, you are his wife.'

'I'm not *his* anything. We're married, that's all. There's no possession in the case.'

'Why *did* you marry him?'

'I wanted a baby.'

'Is that all? Anyone would have done for that.'

'Well, he is anyone, isn't he?'

'You mean—'

'I chose him to be the father of my children. You'd think he'd be flattered—after all, it's a much higher accolade than simply being in love with someone, isn't it?'

'No.'

'Well it should be. But I never loved him—not in the romantic sense. I married him because I wanted a baby, and I think he knew that and resented it. That's why he tried to stop

30

me having one. That was his revenge.'

'Oh Bee!—what do you mean, tried to stop you having one?'

'He would never *try*.'

Clifford's mind boggled. He couldn't think of anything to say. She went on, subdued out of her excitement by the thought.

'And then when I got pregnant anyway, in spite of him, he fixed it his own way.'

'Oh come on, Bee, it wasn't his fault you lost it, was it?'

It was a rhetorical question, but she pushed him hard away from her and sat up, swinging her legs over the side of the bed and turning to glare at him as she answered it.

'Yes, of course it was his fault. I wouldn't have lost that baby. It was perfectly all right. *He* did it. *He did it*.'

'What—'

'He kicked it to death,' she said. 'That's what he did. He kicked me in the belly until the child died, and then it aborted, and destroyed my womb too, so I'll never have another. That's what he did.'

In the silence that followed he heard a car going up the street, running through its gears and fading into the distance.

'Bee—you don't mean it literally?' Clifford pleaded at last. She was hard-eyed, dry-eyed. 'He didn't literally kick you?'

'It was his revenge,' she said. 'He kicked me to make me abort, and now I'll never have a

31

child. A bit extreme really, for revenge.'

'But why didn't you say anything?'

'*Say* anything? To whom? About what? What do you mean *say* anything? To you and Louise? That would make a great topic of conversation over dinner, wouldn't it—how my husband murdered his child.'

'Oh God,' Clifford said weakly. He looked away from her, his hands limp in his lap. In a moment she got up and paced about the room and then said in a normal voice,

'We really must remember to wash out the coffee cups before we go. There's a thick black sludge in the bottom of this one. Want some coffee now?'

'Yes, thanks,' he said automatically. He was thinking of Paul. Of course, Paul did have a temper—you could see it in the way he reacted, and the tense skin around his eyes when he was holding it back—but he couldn't imagine him doing anything as extreme as that. Besides, if he had, surely it would have been noticed at the hospital and reported to the police; there would have been a court case—or at the very least she would surely not have stayed with him, not after such brutality.

And yet he knew perfectly well that battered wives stayed with their husbands for years, so why not Bee? It made no sense. He felt sick, queasy at the thought of it. Could she really mean it literally? If he really had done that, ruined her chances for ever—Lulu had told him that Bee had told her that they had taken away everything but the ovaries, the damage was so bad—she would never have another child, that was sure—my God, that was a terrible thing to do.

What did he know about Bee at all? She was a violent, passionate lover. He could imagine that she might easily have provoked the quick-tempered Paul into a fight, with that horrific result. One thing he knew for certain was that Paul would not do a thing like that deliberately. He loved children and animals, anything small and helpless. He would never have deliberately killed the baby. No, it must have been a fight, and Bee was at least partially responsible for it.

While she waited for the kettle to boil she slipped off her cotton dress and flung it down on the chair. The sight of her nakedness aroused him again. 'Come here,' he said. She walked over to the bed and stood in front of him, and he put his arms round her waist and pulled her to him, resting his face against her belly. She dipped forward and ran her hands over his back lovingly. Right by his eyes there was a mark on her skin, and he lifted his face away, frowning, to look at it. It was a small graze—no, a series of scratches, three vertical, the middle one longer than the outside two, and one horizontal, crossing them. It looked curiously deliberate.

What's this?' he asked her, pointing. She

looked down casually, and away again.

'I don't know. I must have scratched myself on something. It's nothing.' She dropped suddenly to squat and cupped her hands around his organ.

'Hey,' he said, 'what about the coffee.'

'Coffee? What coffee?' she smiled.

'I don't know what you're talking about,' he murmured a moment later. 'I never asked for coffee.'

CHAPTER THREE

Bee and Louise were in the kitchen washing up after dinner, while the men got the cards out and the table and drinks set up. It was a return dinner, though Louise was anxious that it should not seem to be.

'Now that we've got together again, we must make it regular. We mustn't drift apart again. Oh Bee—!' She turned round in sudden affection. Bee regarded her with her head a little on one side. 'It's so *nice* to have you here.'

'All right, Lulu,' Bee said comfortingly. She had the drying cloth in one hand, but Louise at the sink with her yellow-rubber-gloved hands deep in a crusted casserole dish had fallen behind the race and there was nothing to dry. Bee took the high edge of the draining board in the fingers of one hand and executed a few creaking pliés. Louise turned her head again and smiled indulgently.

'Oh Bee, remember the old days, we used to have such fun.'

'When I was Annie Seed and you were Carmen Getme?' Bee asked solemnly. Louise did not always understand what Bee was talking about, and when she did not she usually made it a rule to laugh.

'Do you remember when we did that show, that revue?'

'Every bunch of students puts on a review, trying to rehash *Beyond the Fringe* and falling pitifully far short,' Bee said. 'Ours was every bit as appalling and every bit as much fun to do. Those putrid esoteric jokes—!'

'I think it was jolly good—' Louise began.

'That's it, Lulu. Your choice of adjective tells it all—"jolly good" was about the mark.'

'Oh, you're always so critical. It made a lot of money, anyway. We made over two hundred pounds for Save the Children. Lots of people came.'

'We took ourselves so seriously,' Bee said, swinging her leg horizontally forward and then twisting her body in the opposite direction. Only she knew how stiff it felt, like an uncoiled machine, long unused, long unloved. She had never been loved. Perhaps, she thought, she was unlovable. Oh there's a thought!

'You didn't,' Louise complained a little fretfully. 'You laughed at everything and

35

everyone. You didn't even take finals seriously, though God knows you passed. Don't you remember poor Candy crying her heart out before we went in, and you trotted up whistling and offered her some chewing-gum.' She giggled guiltily and heaved the casserole dish out weightily onto the draining board. 'Don't dry it right away—let it drip for a minute. It's enamel.'

'I never could stand Candy,' Bee said, returning to Louise's side and twirling the drying cloth in her hands. 'What a drip! She was always weeping.'

'I know why you didn't like her—it was because she went out with that new tutor, that nice Dr Whatsisname.'

'Old Walker?' Bee said casually. 'Tommy Walker, the Don with the Luminous Nose.'

'He didn't really drink did he?'

'Of course he did, nonstop. Only he was never drunk, so you infants couldn't tell. Why didn't you ask Candy about it?'

'You see, you *were* jealous of Candy and him,' Louise said triumphantly. Bee looked irritated.

'Oh don't be silly—of course I wasn't jealous. I'd had him long before she—' she stopped suddenly. Louise looked at her with round eyes.

'You didn't.'

'I knew him through Jim—they were at Cambridge together.'

36

'Jim? Oh, Dr Sandys you mean. Bee, did you really have an affair with him?' Louise dropped her voice to confidential level. 'I mean, the whole thing—bed and everything? Did you?'

Bee regarded her with amazement. Louise began to redden slightly.

'Only it was *said*, you know—people *said* you had. Had an affair with him, I mean. And that was why you left in the second year.'

'I came back. I was only ill.'

'I'm sorry, Bee. Only I wondered if you really *did*—and Walker too? Really?'

'Lulu. Oh Lulu.' Bee began to laugh, and after a moment Louise laughed too, not knowing why. Bee flung her arms round Louise's neck and kissed her. Louise caught a hand as it passed her face and said in a worried voice,

'Bee, darling, what on *earth* are all these scratches? Has your cat come back?'

Bee pulled her hand away and regarded the back of it without expression. There were four small patches, each about the size of a sixpence, and in each were several hair-fine scratches. She dropped her hand to her side and detached the other one from Louise.

'I don't know. I expect I got it in the garden. There's a lot of blackberry trailers coming through from the other side of the fence. I think I may ask them if they're going to do anything about that garden, because if they're not I might just offer to go in and dig it all up

37

for them. You can't keep weeds down if they're coming in from next door.'

'You're actually starting to do something there then? I thought you said—'

'I might as well. I have to do something with my life.'

Her voice sounded so bleak that Louise turned to her impulsively and said,

'Bee, darling, don't grieve so. I know it's terrible, but other people live all their lives without children and have very happy lives. I mean, I don't suppose Cliff and I will bother now—we're happy as we are.'

'Yes, that's the difference though, isn't it? You choose not to have any.'

'Yes, but there are lots of advantages, you know. If you have kids you can't have your house looking really nice, and you can't go on lovely holidays abroad, and you can't go out at nights just when you want to. They really do tie you, you know.'

Bee affected not to hear, and executed a few steps across the kitchen floor. Louise's kitchen was tiled with Italian hexagonal tiles with peasantry flowers painted on them. She finished in third position, her head over her shoulder looking at Louise flintily.

'There are lots of things you could do,' Louise went on, trying to be cheerful.

'Such as?' Bee said uncompromisingly.

'Well—' desperately thinking, 'you could take up dancing again.'

'Oh Lulu!' Bee shouted with laughter, dropping her pose and instantly becoming normal and natural, the Bee they had all known and loved. 'I'm thirty years old!'

'Oh well.' Louise shrugged, smiling. 'You can dry that casserole now.'

* * *

In the other room Paul and Clifford were talking about their houses again. It seemed, to Clifford at least, perfectly natural that they should, since it was one of the only two things they had in common. The other was Bee, but Paul didn't know about that.

Paul was talking about his mosaic again. 'You know I didn't want to have anybody official in, but I felt I had to know something about it, so I got onto a chap who's a friend of a chap I know, who does quite a bit in the way of digs and so on—a semi-professional if you follow me. He was actually in on that stuff they dug up a couple of years back in Cirencester, remember?'

'No,' said Clifford, sipping at his after-dinner whisky, but Paul didn't hear, or ignored it.

'Anyway,' he went on, with the slightest tremble of excitement in his voice, 'it turns out that it's even older than we thought—quite excited the chap was. It might be any age.'

'What age is any age?' Clifford asked mildly.

39

Imagine being excited by his kitchen floor when he was not excited by Bee.

'Before the Romans, in any case. He said it was hard to date it because in a sense it's obviously been preserved. But he put me onto a lot of reading about these mazes, and very interesting it's turned out to be.'

'Really?'

'Oh yes. Once you cut through all the religious hoo-ha, of course, because anything odd that's turned up tends to be bunched into religion or fertility rites—sort of archaeological glory-hole, that department. There are any number of these things all over the country—all over the world in fact, various sizes, various ages, but all exactly the same pattern. Usually out of doors, made of little white paths in green lawn, like an ordinary maze in a sense. But what they're for—' Paul shrugged, and after a moment went on, 'I'm getting hold of a book that's quite new. Apparently it puts forward a new theory about them that's very—well, thought-provoking to say the least.'

'And what is it?'

'What's what?'

'The new theory?'

'Oh. I don't know—I haven't seen the book yet. My local library's ordering it for me, but it was only published last week or the week before.'

'Oh,' Clifford said. The conversation lapsed

40

until at last Paul went on in a lower voice, 'I wish I could get Bee interested in it. In anything really. Anything to get her mind off it.'

'How is she?' Clifford asked in exactly the right tone of detached interest. He had been concealing the fact of their relationship from both Louise and Paul for so long that it had become quite effortless. Paul looked first worried, then doubtful, and finally, leaning forward in his chair, evidently determined to confide.

'She's been behaving very strangely,' he said. 'I'm very worried about her, you know, Cliff. Listen, do you think she might be—well, mentally sick?'

'We all are, more or less,' Clifford said evasively, without even considering the question. He habitually took Paul less than seriously, perhaps for the very reason that he was having an affair with his wife. It made the deception more tolerable.

'No, seriously,' Paul protested mildly. 'I have wondered, recently, if she might really be going round the bend.'

'Bee was always at least half way round the bend; it wouldn't take much of a shove to send her the rest of the way.'

Paul was hurt. 'I'm not joking.'

Clifford allowed himself to look grave. 'Nor was I.' There was evidently no help for it. 'All right, what makes you think she's any worse than before?'

'I don't know, really,' Paul said, typically. 'It's just that she seems different. Strange. She seems like a different person sometimes. She wanders about a lot at night. And she's always banging into things. She never used to be clumsy but now she's always covered in bruises and scratches.'

There was nothing there, but all the same Clifford saw that Paul was waiting for an answer. He said, 'I don't think there's anything seriously wrong with her, but she may be having a sort of nervous breakdown, a mild one, as a result of—' Knowing what he knew. Clifford couldn't go on. He averted his face and finished off his whisky. 'Can I get you another drink?'

Paul shook his head vaguely, his face creased with thought. 'I can understand her being upset over losing the baby—Christ, who wouldn't be? But I don't see why that should turn her against me. It wasn't my fault she lost it, and yet sometimes she seems really to hate me.'

Clifford jerked to his feet and walked a few paces about the room, and then came back to face Paul angrily. He hadn't meant to reveal what he knew, but he couldn't stop himself.

'You don't have to put on that innocent act with me,' he said in a low voice. 'I know all about the—fight you had that day.'

'Fight?' Paul seemed bewildered. 'What

fight? What are you talking about?'

'You want me to spell it out? I know about the fight you had the day she aborted, and how you kicked her. So wash out all that "not my fault" stuff.'

'Cliff, have you gone potty? We didn't have a fight. What on earth made you think we had? *Kicked* her? You don't really think I would— Christ, Cliff, what do you take me for?'

There was no denying that he sounded genuine. He seemed both surprised and shocked, the natural reaction if he were innocent. Clifford sat down again and regarded him steadily.

'Who told you that stuff?' Paul asked now, an angry edge to his voice.

'Bee believes it,' he said.

'*She* told you that?'

Clifford hesitated. It seemed unlikely that Bee would tell him something like that if their relationship was only what it was meant to seem. He said finally, 'Bee told Louise and she told me. Don't tell her I broke her confidence, will you?'

Paul waved his hands vaguely. 'She really believes that?'

'So it seems.'

'Then she must be going mad. I mean, really mad.'

'Look, why don't you tell me exactly what happened that day?'

'All right, if only to put you straight. Well, it

43

happened in the middle of the night, of course—'

'No, tell me from the beginning. It was a Sunday, wasn't it? What did you do all day?'

'Nothing at all, just the usual Sunday things. She was beginning to get big then, so we didn't do anything energetic on Sundays any more. We had late breakfast, read the papers in the garden, walked down to the river and back in the afternoon, dinner—cooked by me— watched a bit of telly, and then went to bed. All perfectly normal.'

'And then?'

'I went to sleep. Bee was a bit restless—she got up a couple of times, but then she often did. She still does, in fact. Then about three in the morning I woke up and she was screaming.' He paused and swallowed. 'She was sitting up in bed screaming, and flailing her arms about in front of her as if she was fighting someone off. I sat up and switched on the light, and then I saw the blood. There seemed to be an awful lot of it. So I rang for an ambulance. And that was it really.' He looked across at Clifford. 'You believe me, don't you?'

Clifford nodded. He had never felt happy about the other version anyway, and Paul's sincerity was evident. He said at last, 'I wonder if she had a nightmare—waving her arms about, you said, as if she was fighting someone—and that's what she remembers?'

'But surely she ought to know the difference

between a nightmare and what really happens?'

Clifford shrugged. 'Normally, yes.'

'Do you think I ought to get medical help? Take her to a psychiatrist or something?'

Clifford made a gesture of warding off with his hand. 'That's not for me to say, old boy. You must decide for yourself. I don't want to influence you in a matter like that.' Paul accepted that without protest. 'I must say I haven't noticed anything particularly deranged about her.'

Paul was still thinking. 'I think I'll consult her doctor about her, quietly, without saying anything to her. We can't go on like this, anyway. God knows I love her, but she's becoming more and more strange every day.'

'That's for you to decide,' Clifford said. 'Let's change the subject—they'll be in any moment.'

So they had ended up discussing Bee after all. Oh well, that's life.

*   *   *

Louise and Paul met in the suitably anonymous surroundings of the Oxford Circus Woolworths. Louise worked in Cavendish Square, and Paul in Bond Street, so it suited them both to have lunch together there several times a week; and it was highly unlikely they would meet anyone they knew there. They carried their trays over to a small table by the window that had only two seats, and felt lucky for the privacy.

Paul caught Louise up on the latest development.

'And he said *I* told him?' Louise said, puzzled.

'That's what he said. He said Bee told you and you told him.'

'Well I certainly didn't. I mean, Bee never told me anything of the sort. What on earth can he be on about?'

'Do you think he made it up?'

'Well, it's a very strange thing to make up, isn't it? I mean, that's practically libellous, isn't it? Saying you kicked poor Bee—I just don't know what to think. It's very odd.'

'Well, do you think Bee told him, then? He said she really believed it.'

'I suppose she must have, though I can't think when she could have found the time.'

'Oh, I don't know. We've been together enough these last couple of weeks, haven't we?'

'Yes, but all together.'

'But there's often times when one or other of us is out of the room.'

'I suppose so.' She considered. 'But why would she tell *him* that? Do you think she was trying to turn him against you for some reason?'

'I shouldn't think so. Cliff said she really believed it.'

'Well, he hardly knows her well enough to judge her private motivations. I mean, he said he hadn't noticed anything odd about her behaviour, and even *I've* noticed that.'

'Noticed what?'

'That she's behaving oddly,' Louise said impatiently. 'Sort of erratic and jumpy. She says odd things and laughs.'

Paul reserved comment on that. Bee had always said odd things and laughed. The fact was a lot of the things she said were cryptic quotations and allusions, and Louise, bless her heart, was not always quick enough or bright enough to solve the puzzle.

'What really worried me is the way she's knocking herself about.'

Louise's eyes grew very wide. 'Paul! What on earth can you mean?'

'Well, she's always coming up with these bruises and scratches. I haven't seen her do it, but when I ask her about them she says she fell over or bumped into something. She never used to be clumsy like that. One bruise every now and then I could understand—everyone bangs into things sometimes—but she's got a couple of new ones every day.'

Louise giggled suddenly. 'You don't think she's having an affair with a sadist.'

Paul frowned. 'I don't think that's funny.'

'Oh, come on, Paul, it was only a joke. Don't be so stiff. Look, I'm worried about poor Bee too, but after all, you have to expect it when

47

she's had such a shock. She'll get over it, but it might be some time. I remember reading in a magazine that it can take five years to get over losing a child.'

'That's not a lot of comfort,' Paul said gloomily.

*   *   *

Bee was re-potting geraniums. She padded barefoot into the kitchen for some more water, and half way across stopped and lifted her foot sharply, like a cat.

'Yeuk!' she said automatically, and then glancing down saw that it was only water. But what a lot of it. Where could it be coming from? There was a pool in the middle of the floor and, because of the slight slope on the floor it was slowly working its way towards the sink.

She went and had a look at the fridge, thinking it might have somehow turned itself off and be defrosting, but all seemed well within. She stood still, puzzling. Had she spilled something? She glanced up—no stain on the ceiling. Oh well, she had better wipe it up, anyway. She got the floor cloth from under the sink and knelt down by the puddle and mopped it up, moving her hand in wide, circular sweeps. There was so much of it she had to keep getting up and going to the sink to wring out the cloth.

'Gives the floor a clean, anyway,' she said aloud. As she got up the last time she felt suddenly dizzy—it reminded her of the days when she was pregnant, and any sudden movement would send the blood rushing away from her head, and everything would go black and red and there would be a ringing, singing in her ears. She must have got up too quickly. She ducked her head and shook it, feeling the heavy, throbbing pressure on her eardrums. She moved to the sink and gripped it with one hand while the other she dropped the cloth into the sink and ran the tap on it to rinse it out. She must still have been dizzy, because for a second the rinsings running out of the cloth looked dark red, like blood.

*　　*　　*

Clifford and Louise generally did all their bedtime things and then came back downstairs in dressing-gowns for a nightcap. Usually they watched the late news on the television or, if it was very late, switched on to the World Service bulletin. Louise was evidently distracted tonight, for she paid no attention to the hints of a general election or the threatened car-workers strike that could pretty well put paid to Britain's family car industry; she fidgeted, and picked at her nails. At last she said,

'Clifford, what were you and Paul talking about the other night when we were doing the

49

washing-up?'

She wanted desperately to know why he had told Paul that strange thing, but she couldn't very well reveal to him that she knew about it, without also revealing that she met Paul for lunch. She had never told Cliff that, from the fear—or perhaps hope—that he would be jealous and make a fuss about it.

'Hm?' Clifford said vaguely. He heard the question all right but would rather not answer it, so he kept his eyes fixed on the newscaster with the air of one whose attention is fully occupied.

'I said—'

'Bee,' Clifford said irritably. 'We were talking about Bee. Or rather he was. I was listening.'

'What about her?'

'Look, Lulu, I'm trying to hear the news.'

'You've heard it before,' Louise said reasonably. 'I'm interested in Bee. She is my friend, my best friend. Do you think she—'

'Oh God,' Clifford forestalled her wearily. 'Does nobody talk about anything else any more? I shouldn't be surprised if they start giving out bulletins on the nine-o'clock-news next. And little notes on the front gate: "Mrs Hague had a comfortable night".'

'You don't have to be rude,' Louise said, hurt.

'I do have to be rude. I don't want to talk about the Hagues, and especially not about

50

Bee's readjustment problems. All right?'

'All right,' Louise said, folding her lips tight.

Later in bed she whispered, 'Clifford, are you still awake?'

'Mm?' he replied, feigning deep sleep.

'Cliff—' a long pause. 'Cliff, do you want us to have children? Not now, I mean, but in the future? We've never spoken about it, and I've just assumed you didn't want any, but—'

'No.'

'No what?'

'No, I don't want any.'

'Oh.' She hadn't expected so blunt an answer. 'But supposing I'd wanted some?'

'Why suppose?'

'Well, if you say quite categorically you don't, but what if—'

'Lulu,' he interrupted her firmly.

'Yes?'

'Do you want children?'

'No—but.'

'Just "No" is enough. You don't want children. I don't want children. We haven't got any children. We shan't have any children. All right? Good. Go to sleep.'

Louise sighed heavily. 'I just said what if,' she said, but quietly, to herself. She was soon asleep. Clifford, on the other hand, lay wakeful, breathing regularly to make Louise think he was asleep too. He was thinking of Louise and Beatrice and children. No, Lulu, I don't want any. But had it been Bee—children

51

are where love naturally tends. The answer would have been different if he had had the sense to marry Bee when she was free. But of course, when she was free he hadn't been in love with her. And when he'd found her again and fallen in love with her, she'd been married to Paul. And now none of them would ever have any children.

CHAPTER FOUR

'Listen to this bit, Bee,' Paul said. He was reading the book that the library had got for him, and every now and then tried to share a bit with Bee. She was sitting across from him, curled up in one corner of the sofa crocheting. He liked to see her doing something like that—it was so womanly. Her fingers flew deftly, and she didn't even seem to have to look at them. It was feminine and good, the sort of thing a happy wife did. Bee had too often seemed to him hard, harsh, unwomanly. When he glanced at her he smiled to himself. 'Listen to this bit: *"It is now very widely held that homing pigeons and migrating birds find their way by following lines of magnetic force along the earth's surface. This has been shown by experiment. Birds with their eyes, ears or nose covered could still find their way, but birds to whom a small magnet had been fixed merely flew purposelessly in circles. The implication was clear: the magnet had interfered with their perception of the earth's magnetic fields".'*

He glanced across at Bee, who, feeling his look, looked up also.

'Mm?' she said vaguely.

'Bee, were you listening?' he said reproachfully.

'Yes, about homing pigeons,' she said distractedly. She appeared to be listening for something.

'What's up, darling?' Paul asked her, closing the book. He found it impossible to interest her in anything these days. The book on the mazes was so fascinating he thought she'd bound to take an interest: but she seemed to be growing vaguer and vaguer. Nervy, too—she started violently at any sound or movement. Once when he had gone into the kitchen and come up behind her she had jumped nearly out of her skin and burst into tears.

'Nothing,' she said now, a little too hastily. He looked at her more closely to see if she'd been crying, and saw that she hadn't; but saw also how haggard she was getting. The black dress she was wearing had fitted her snugly—a little too snugly at one time. Now it was loose, and her bare arms looked thin. On the left one, on the rounded part of the upper arm, there was a bruise.

'Bee, you would tell me if there was something wrong, wouldn't you?' he asked her

53

now. 'I mean, you do feel that you could tell me, don't you?'

She looked up at him expressionlessly. Then her right hand freed itself from the crochet work and began brushing at her skirt, as if she was brushing something off it. He had seen her do that before, too.

'You know don't you,' he went on more quietly, 'that I love you?' He found it very difficult to say things like that. He had never been able to talk about his feelings to her; but he felt now that it was necessary. He had the sense that something was going on that he didn't know about, that she was keeping something from him. Yet he was afraid to confront her with what he thought: he was afraid that she really would turn out to be mad, that she would do something that would confirm his suspicions. He didn't want them confirmed. He wanted her to be well again.

She did not answer any of his questions. Instead, still brushing at her skirt, she said, 'Read me some more of the book.'

He recognised this for what it was—a blatant attempt to turn him from the subject. He put the book down and came over to her and squatted in front of her so that their eyes were almost on a level. Hers seemed very black and deep and expressionless, like water in the dark.

'Darling,' he began. He didn't know what to say. He caught her brushing hand in his and stroked it. Then, 'What's that in your hair?' He said it only for something to say, but he felt her instant reaction—she went rigid, and her face stiffened. She had always been afraid of spiders, and he thought she took his words that way.

'It's all right, darling, it's nothing nasty,' he said, smiling, 'it's just some—petals, it looks like. Yes—look, little white petals.' He picked them out, half a dozen tiny white petals, beginning to brown, like the petals of hawthorn flowers. He showed them to her in the palm of his hand, and her rigid body seemed to arch away from them. He was contrite. 'Darling, I didn't mean to startle you. I'm sorry.'

'It's—all right,' she said with an obvious effort. Then, gaining strength, 'You know how I am about—insects.'

'Yes of course,' he said generously, though he could see from the whiteness of her face how shocked she had been. 'How about a little drink? In the way of a nightcap?' She nodded and he got up and went towards the door.

'I'll get it,' she said. He was already at the door.

'No, it's all right, Bee, I'll go.'

'I'll get it!' she cried, and there was an edge of hysteria in her voice. He paused, considering, and then said soothingly, 'All right, dear. I'll have a whisky.'

She said nothing more, but got up and

55

walked unsteadily to the door. As she moved another couple of petals fell from her, from amongst her clothing perhaps, and fluttered to the floor. When she had gone out he picked them up and threw them with the others into the grate.

Bee went to the dining-room and got out the whisky bottle. The petals had shaken her badly. She had found the first of them two days before in the passage. Then, yesterday, there were some up the stairs, and when she went to make the bed, they were between the sheets, dozens of them, practically a bedfull. She didn't know where they came from. She had been at first puzzled, then frightened. She had believed that they were a figment of her imagination, and she had been frightened to think she was going mad. Now Paul had seen them too, and instead of being reassured she was even more frightened. If they were real—what then?

She put the whisky bottle and the two glasses onto the silver drinks tray, a wedding present from her godmother. Whimpering, she picked another petal off the tray and crushed it between her finger nails as one might try to crush a flea. Then she took the glass water-jug to the kitchen to fill it.

She paused at the doorway. Surprising how loud the 'fridge sounded at night. Its engine droned quite audibly. She stepped down into the kitchen and at once it grew louder so that

56

she could almost feel it as well as hear it. She crossed quickly to the sink, ignoring it, trying to keep her mind on what she was doing. Water, water, jug, jug, tap, tap. Fill jug water tap. Water, whisky, nightcap, Paul. Paul. PAUL!

Paul came running as she began to scream, moving faster than he had ever moved in his life. He heard the water-jug smash on the kitchen floor as her screams ran into each other and became one long, nerve-shattering shriek. As he reached the kitchen door he saw her standing at the sink. The tap was running, she was staring into the sink and screaming. His first thought was that there was a spider in the sink, his second, as he reached her, that she had cut herself, for her hand was hanging over the sink, her fingers downwards, touching the surface of the liquid; the liquid was deep red; the sink was full of blood.

* * *

'It's all right, Bee, it's all right. Hush now. Everything's all right.'

Bee was sitting on one of the dining-room chairs, whence he had half-carried her. He had forced some whisky through her clenched, chattering teeth, and now she was merely sobbing, her body limp against his surrounding arm.

'You saw it. You saw it too!'

'I thought I saw it—'

'It was blood, it was blood!' she whimpered in terror.

'Darling, it wasn't. It was water. It came out of the tap, Bee, it was ordinary old plain tap-water. It was just for a minute the way the light caught it that made it look red, and just for a minute you thought something very silly. Look at me, darling; now, it was water—all right? You do believe me?'

'Paul—' her voice quivered.

'It was a shock, coming on top of the fact that you've not been sleeping very well. It was just the way the light caught it. All right, darling?'

'Yes,' she whispered. She gave a shaky sigh and leaned back against him. 'Oh Paul, I've been so scared.'

'I know, darling, but it's all right now. Have some more whisky.'

She tried to laugh. 'Are you trying to get me drunk?'

'That's my good, brave girl. Come on, drink up your whisky, and we'll go up to bed.'

He felt her stiffen instantly, saw the reaction of fear in her eyes.

'What is it, darling?'

'Paul—make sure there's nothing in the bed.'

'Oh Bee, really—'

'*Please*, Paul—please. Please have a look first, and make sure there's no—nothing—in

58

the—'

'All right, darling. Don't be afraid. Come on now, bring your whisky with you, and you shall see me search the bed thoroughly.'

They walked upstairs together. Bee leaned against him as they mounted the stairs, and he felt her light, lighter than before. Was she losing much weight, he wondered? Perhaps that might be an excuse to get her to a doctor. In the bedroom she stood back a little way and watched, rigidly attentive, as he stripped back the sheet and examined each crevice and fold of the bedclothes. There was nothing there, not so much as a bit of fluff.

'All right darling? Satisfied?'

She nodded, and, putting the whisky down by her bedside table she shakily undressed herself and got into bed. He made her drink the rest of it before he put off the light and they settled down to sleep. His mind relaxed slowly and drifted over the evening and all the other strange things that Bee had done and said recently. His last thought before he fell asleep was:

'Hawthorn petals? In August?'

But by the next morning he had forgotten it completely.

* * *

Clifford was obviously in a bad mood. He felt irritable, and all his answers to her, from the

59

time they met, right through lunch and up to the bedsitter, were sharp. At last, when they had undressed, it exploded.

'For God's sake,' he said, catching her by the arm and turning her round roughly, 'What are all these bloody bruises? It's like trying to screw with a female wrestler. Why in hell have you started walking into things all of a sudden?'

She stared at him sullenly.

'You're in a charming mood, I must say.'

'I am? You've been a little ray of sunshine yourself for some time past.'

'Possibly. But at least I have the grace not to bring my moods up here with me. What's the matter with you—Louise been giving you trouble?'

'Bitchiness doesn't suit you, my dear—'

'Don't "my dear" me, you hypocritical bastard. You only "my dear" when you're about to say something particularly nasty.' It was an effort at conciliation—he ought to have laughed at it, but he didn't. So she went on, 'Would you mind letting go of my arm? You're hurting me.'

'Well, you should enjoy that, by all accounts. Have you developed masochistic tendencies so late in life? Have nice little flagellation sessions with yourself while Paul's at work?'

'You're hurting me,' she repeated woodenly.

'Oh well, that'll give you another nice bruise, won't it? You should enjoy that.'

'I can't help the bruises. I don't do it on purpose,' she said, and tears sprang to her eyes. He shook her, still gripping so that his fingers dug almost to the bone.

'Don't do what on purpose? What do you do to get these lovely bruises?'

'I don't do anything,' she protested. 'They just come.'

'They just come?' he mocked. He shook her again. 'And you can stop forcing tears into your eyes—I'm not affected. What do you mean, they just come?'

'What I say, blast you. One minute they're not there, and next they are.'

'Oh yes,' he said deridingly. She shouted at him,

'Think what you like, you pig! And let me go! You're bloody hurting me, I tell you!'

'But you like it—you like being hurt. Bruises don't just come—you do it yourself.'

'They do. I wake up with them in the morning.'

'Oho, now we're getting to it. Paul beats you up at nights while you're asleep, does he?'

'No. Yes. I don't know. All I know is they're there in the morning when I wake up. I don't know how they get there.'

'Well, Paul's well known as a wife beater, isn't he? After all, he kicked your baby to death, didn't he?'

Bee was weeping now, struggling to release her arm. 'Yes,' she choked.

61

'Liar!' he shouted, and he hit her across the face with his free hand. She screamed, and began to struggle in earnest now. 'I told him what you'd said, and he said it was all lies. He didn't touch you. You woke up in the middle of the night bleeding. He didn't lay a finger on you. It was all lies from beginning to end.'

'You told him!'

'Oh yes, that shocks you, doesn't it.'

'You told him I'd told you?'

'No, I told him you told Louise. And he denied it.'

'Of course he denied it, you bloody fool. Do you think he'd admit it? Let me go, damn you.'

'He denied it because it wasn't true,' Clifford shouted, and he hit her again, letting go of her arm at the same time so that the blow knocked her across the tiny room and she fell on the bed. She struggled up, screaming incoherently, and flew at him. He was amazed by her strength. She grappled with him, and her teeth were at his neck, trying to reach his jugular. He was really frightened, frightened out of his rage, and he seized her shoulders and forced her back, keeping her head as far back from him as possible. Her face was contorted with rage and she was screaming at him,

'You won't do it, you won't do it, you filthy swine! I'll kill you first!'

'Bee, stop, Bee, stop,' he cried, suddenly sobered, afraid of what he might have induced by his temper. There was a clamorous

62

knocking on the door, and a man's voice shouted through to them.

'What's going on in there? Pack it in, or I'll call the police! What are you doing? Come on, open this door! Open it, or I'll have the law on you.'

'Bee, please, Bee, stop please,' Clifford begged her. She glared at him, then focussed, then began to relax while the knocking went on outside. When she went limp he let her subside on the bed, and went to the door, opening it a crack. Instantly weight was thrown on it from the outside, and it was forced open. A large man in braces stood there, holding a poker.

'What the hell's going on?' he demanded angrily, though Clifford could see the fear behind the anger. 'Sounded like blue bloody murder. You can't make a row like that here. What've you been doing to her?'

'It was just a quarrel,' Clifford said mildly.

'Didn't sound like a bloody quarrel. What's wrong with her? If there's been funny business here I'm going for the police, I don't care who you are, with your fancy accent.'

'Just a quarrel,' Clifford said, pushing the door back. He was hidden from the waist down behind it, but naked Bee was exposed on the bed, and was only just gathering herself enough to pull a blanket across herself. 'Sorry we made a noise. We won't do it again. All right?'

'No, it ain't all right. Look at them bruises

63

on her. I'm going for the police!' He turned about in the doorway and Clifford threw an appealing glance at Bee, who roused herself enough to say,

'No, no, it's all right. I got those bruises in a car crash. I smashed my car up yesterday. It's nothing to do with him. We were just having a quarrel. It's all right now, honestly. I'm all right.'

The man turned again, suspicious but glad to be mollified.

'Well, if you're sure.'

Bee tried a watery smile. 'Oh yes, I'm all right. It was nice of you to be worried, but it was nothing.'

Half flattered, half righteous, he backed off. 'Well, all I can say is, keep the noise down another time. Bloody hell, it sounded like a murder. We don't want that kind of racket round here. There are decent people living in this house, and don't you forget it.'

With Clifford urging the door at him, he backed away, unconvinced but glad not to have to take further action. The door closed, and for a moment there was silence. Then Clifford turned towards Bee, still lying on the bed.

'Bee,' he began appealingly.

'You hit me,' she accused harshly.

'You were hysterical,' he countered.

'That's not why you hit me.'

That was true. 'I'm sorry,' he said

64

awkwardly. She raised an eyebrow, and he admitted the inadequacy of the apology. It came over him in sweeps of remorse what he had done and said. 'Oh Bee. Oh Christ I'm sorry. I don't know what came over me. Just for a minute I really hated you, I wanted to kill you. I don't understand it. You know I wouldn't hurt you, I wouldn't hurt a hair on your head. I love you. Oh God, can you ever forgive me?'

'I don't understand it either. I don't understand any of what's happening. What made you do it, Cliff?'

'I don't know. I don't know.' They stared at each other for a moment. 'Bee, who did you think I was?'

'Eh?'

'You were shouting at me, I won't do it, I'll kill you first. Do what? Who were you shouting at?'

'I didn't say that.'

'You did.'

'I don't remember saying it. You imagined it.'

'I didn't. You said it.' She stared at him and he stared impassively back. She moved nervously. 'Don't Cliff. Don't do that. I'm afraid—I'm afraid my memory's going. I remember things that haven't happened. And now you say I did something I don't remember.'

Clifford seized the idea with relief. 'But if

that's the case--it would explain—I'm sorry Bee, but I have to bring it up again—the business of the question over how you lost that baby. I know, I'm sorry,' as she made a gesture of weariness with the subject, 'but look—I spoke to Paul about it, and he said you went to bed as usual, and he woke in the night and it was happening. Just like that. No interference from him. And I believed him—no, listen! I believed him. But I also believe that you firmly believe he kicked you.'

'He kicked me,' Bee said in a low voice. 'He did it.'

'Well, you see, if it's your memory playing you tricks, that accounts for it. No-one's a liar, no-one's a villain. Just a little nervous reaction from you after the terrible shock you've had.'

Bee stared down at her hands, her head bent like one defeated. Clifford watched her and felt a giant tenderness for her that was even then part lust. Why did she affect him so profoundly? She stirred at the roots of his being with every movement, every word.

She said, very low, 'I don't want that to be the answer. If that's what it is, then it isn't a little thing. I'm afraid. Cliff, am I going mad? Is that what it is?'

'No,' he said emphatically—too emphatically. He crossed to the bed and sat down beside her, taking her hand. He had seen Fonteyn dance *Swan Lake* once, and there was just a movement when, on their first meeting,

66

the Prince takes up the Swan's thin, limp hand, to draw her to her feet. Always demanding: love, the man, demanding of the woman until she has given everything, until she is sucked dry and dies. Even when he gives it is a form of final demand. Even in his tenderness, his pity for her, he could not leave her alone. He wanted to have her.

She looked up wearily, recognising the supplication in his sympathy, and responded to it obediently, obediently to her nature; but she said,

'I think I am. But even that's better than the alternative.'

CHAPTER FIVE

They were all walking along by the river, taking their Sunday afternoon constitutional, before going back to Bee and Paul's for dinner. Already there was the presence of autumn in the evidence of all the senses. Though sunny, it was cool. Some leaves—admittedly still green—had fallen and the small wind carried that scent which is either blackberries or woodsmoke. They strolled in pairs. Paul and Louise had got ahead, walking more vigorously. Bee and Clifford lagged behind, walking as though it were their last hour together. Cliff had picked up a stick and he

67

slashed idly at the grass as he moved; Bee had her hands in the pockets of her blazer and watched the point of the stick as it swung to and fro as a kitten watches the end of a knitting needle in action and prepares to spring.

'What do you suppose they're talking about?' Clifford asked idly, for want of something to say.

'Paul and Lulu?' She looked at them and smiled. 'I know exactly what they're talking about. Look at Paul's hands, what do you think he's describing?'

'Swiss roll manufacture?' Clifford hazarded. Bee snorted derisively.

'The maze, of course. I'm beginning to wish we'd never uncovered it. It's a mania with him. This new book he's got has made him worse than ever.'

'What did the new theory turn out to be?'

'Oh, you heard about it did you?'

'He told me he was getting the book, but I haven't had selected quotations from it yet.'

'You will. Perhaps I shouldn't spoil your anticipation.'

'Give me the gist in not more than thirty-five words. That way I can stop listening and still make intelligent noises.'

'You are a cruel pig. I shouldn't let you talk that way about my husband. Not in front of me anyway.'

'It doesn't matter,' Clifford said, sounding weary. 'Nothing you say will change my opinion of him or of your marriage to him. You don't need to feel disloyal.'

'I don't know about loyalty. What should one pay it to? Should the recipient earn it, or does it come as part of the relationship, like the bulb in a lamp?'

'Christ, *I* don't know,' Clifford said. 'Why ask me? I've never even felt loyal towards myself. I don't know what it means.'

'Tush! You don't fool me,' Bee said, narrowing her eyes. 'You put on this Flashman act every now and then, but I know you're true blue underneath.'

'Believe what you like, my dear,' he said. 'I simply warn you not to rely on me to catch you when you jump from a burning house.' He touched her wrist briefly, and her hand disentangled itself from her pocket to hold his. 'Well, what's this 'mazing theory, then?'

She didn't notice the pun. 'Briefly, the idea is that the earth is a huge magnet, and that the earth's surface is covered in lines of magnetic force. And these mazes are built where various lines intersect. Like an interchange station on the underground.'

He waited. 'Is that it?'

'Uh-huh.'

'But what are they *for*?'

'How would I know? I think there's some idea that they might have been some way of tapping the energy—sort of like dynamos or something—but what *for* I couldn't tell you. I

69

don't suppose Paul could tell you, and he's read all there is to read. It's like Stonehenge all over again.'

'I thought Stonehenge was a temple?'

'Don't say that to Paul,' Bee warned, grinning. 'He's likely to blow a fuse. Dolmens are apparently another form of whatever the mazes are. Oh, and so is the Bermuda Triangle.'

'Quite. The fun is in asking the questions, not in getting the answers.'

They walked on in silence for a while until they saw the others turn back. Then they stopped to let them catch up.

'We'd better be getting back or we won't have time for something I want to show you,' Paul said as they came up to them. Bee and Clifford exchanged a grin. The four of them fell into line, Bee and Cliff on the inside, Louise next to Cliff and Paul next to Bee. Clifford felt comfortable, at ease. Bee's hand was still in his—they had established enough innocent friendliness for this to pass without comment—and Louise was on his other arm. It was beginning to get dark. Paul hurried them, and they let him, indulgently.

Clifford, in closest physical contact with Bee, noticed how she changed as they drew nearer the house. It was gradual, but slowly she grew more tense, her steps dragging a little in reluctance to complete the journey. She dropped out of the conversation, and answered only in monosyllables when pressed. When they turned into their street she withdrew her hand from his sharply, and glancing at her he was shocked at the apprehension in her face.

'Bee?' he asked her softly. She threw a look at him sideways, showing the whites of her eyes like an animal. Paul now also noticed the change, and tried to take her other hand.

'It's all right, darling,' he said. 'I'll go in first.' He saw Clifford's enquiring glance and said with an effort, 'She's been scared by a couple of outsize spiders. Now she thinks they're round every corner. I have to make sure there's nothing there before she'll go in.'

It was palpably a lie, but Clifford did not know what it was designed to conceal. He glanced at Louise, and saw from her expression of mixed smugness and concern that whatever the secret was, she was in on it. That was odd. Why had Paul told her and not him?

They reached the house and now Bee was obviously dragging back, though she seemed to do it against her own will. Paul opened the door with his key and stepped in confidently, putting on the hall light. He walked straight in without looking back to see if they were following, went right to the end of the passage and came back again.

'It's all right,' he said briefly. Bee looked at him searchingly, and seemed not to be comforted, but she walked in after him, stepping over the threshold with the white showing all round her eyes. Louise fell in behind her, and Clifford came last, closing the front door behind him. As he walked down the corridor in the others' wake he heard that heavy vibrating noise he had heard before.

'What's that?' he asked sharply, affected by the general tension.

'Aircraft,' Paul said promptly. 'A big one, high up.'

'No it's not,' said Bee, and he was amazed by how calm she sounded. 'It's the 'fridge's motor. I was surprised how loud it sounded when the house was quiet. But you can tell, it comes from the kitchen, not outside.'

The noise subsided, but did not seem, to Clifford, to stop entirely, merely to fall below the level of hearing. It was as if a dog, roused by an intruder to snarl, had dropped his voice to a low uneasy growl.

'Bee, would you like to fix the drinks?' Paul called cheerfully over his shoulder. 'I'm getting the dinner tonight,' he added in explanation.

'Don't be fooled,' Bee said with an effort at fun. 'It sounds as though he's going to be donning an apron and slaving over a hot stove for a couple of hours. Actually we're having salad and a cold sweet, so he's only got to put it on the table.'

'Giving away all my trade secrets—have you no loyalty, wife?' Paul shouted back from the kitchen. Bee and Clifford did not look at each

72

other.

'What would anyone like to drink?' she asked instead.

They took their drinks into the twilit drawing-room and made desultory conversation. Everyone was affected by the mood of apprehension which Bee had brought into the house with her. Louise and Clifford were both thinking, though unknown to each other, that it was time something was done about Bee, that it was time she sought professional help, for she was getting worse instead of better. She was making a brave attempt to behave naturally now, but she fidgeted in her seat, looking around her all the time as if she expected to be jumped on, and making a futile brushing movement at her clothes and hair every now and then.

They were all glad when Paul came in to claim his drink.

'Right, now it's all laid out, so we can start any time we like. But before we do, I want to perform a little parlour trick.'

'Oh yes?' said Clifford, unencouragingly. Bee said nothing, merely stared at the floor, and Louise smiled and said,

'What is it, indoor fireworks?'

'Fireworks all right, I hope, but only metaphorically. You know I've been trying to find out more about mazes, and there's a theory currently that they are something to do with the earth's magnetic field.' Clifford looked at Bee to wink at her, but she would not look up. 'Well, yesterday I went out and bought some iron filings, and I'm going to try a little experiment that I read about in this book.' He tapped it on the cover, and held up with his other hand, just like an amateur conjurer, an ironmonger's brown packet.

'Iron filings—that takes me back,' Louise said. 'The very first experiment we did in chemistry at school was with iron filings and powdered sulphur.'

'Well, shall we go?' Paul said, a little impatient with the lack of enthusiasm for what he had prepared for them.

'All right, let's get it over with,' Clifford said with exaggerated tolerance so that Paul would think he was joking.

They walked in Indian file down to the kitchen, and assembled on the step looking down while Paul took up his position on the stage.

'Ladees and gentlemen,' he began, 'Pree-senting, for your amazement, amusement and utter astonishment, thee most ree-markable—'

'Oh get on with it,' Bee snapped, and there was a pause at her evident bad humour.

'Okay,' he said mildly. 'Watch.'

In the few seconds before there was anything to see, Clifford listened for the humming noise, and couldn't catch it at all, though he had the feeling that it was there, like a presence. Then his attention was riveted as Paul poured the iron filings in a wide sweep over the mosaic of the maze. They fell like dark snow over the white and green chips and then, a split second later, began to move of their own accord, writhing and wriggling about in a horribly live fashion. Louise was reminded of the tortured writhing of custard powder when once she had by mistake spilled hot water on it.

Clifford was conscious of Bee's indrawn breath, and of Paul's satisfied smirk—he had known what to expect. Then the show was over. The filings had been scattered haphazardly; they had moved themselves so that they lay neatly along the white lines of the maze, making a dark grey stripe down the centre of the curving paths.

'By God,' Clifford said.

'It's fantastic,' Louise said. 'That's magnetism, is it?'

'Something like,' Paul said happily. Bee made no comment.

'You knew what would happen?' Clifford asked, and Paul gave a sheepish grin.

'I had a little practice here yesterday when Bee was out. Noting worse than a conjuring trick that goes wrong. Fascinating, isn't it? The magnetic field must be really pretty strong. I'd seen something like it done at school, with a tray full of iron filings, and you draw pictures in them by moving a magnet about under the tray. Then I read about tests in this book of mine. Thought I'd try it out. Weird the way

75

they move on their own, isn't it? Wriggling like tadpoles.'

'I once—' Louse began to tell about her experience with the custard powder, but she was stopped by a most peculiar sound from Bee. They turned to stare at her. It was getting dark now, and the light was not yet on in the kitchen. In the light Bee's face was as white as a lily on a deep pond—stark white and floating in the half-darkness. Her eyes were shut, and she looked as though she were going to faint, but she made a strange moaning noise, very low and rough in the throat.

'Bee—' Paul said, making a move towards her. She spoke then, turning her closed eyes towards him as if she could see through the lids.

'You couldn't leave it alone. You have to interfere. Now it will all start again. All the blood and fear and pain. Why wouldn't you leave us alone?'

'Bee—what is it darling? What's the matter?' He reached out for her, but some instinct made Clifford catch Paul's hand and hold it back. It seemed to him she shouldn't be touched. Perhaps it was some almost forgotten reading about the danger of interfering with mediums; he didn't know why he did it. Her voice did not sound like hers—it was rough and harsh, almost as if she were not used to speaking, or as if this were not her own tongue.

She moaned again, and then her eyes flew

76

open. She stared around her in terror, looking past Clifford and Louise as if they were not there. Her eyes fixed on Paul, standing a few feet from her with his feet amongst the iron filings, and as they did her face contorted with fury and hatred and fear.

'You!' she choked. 'You did it! You! The blood is on your head, the death of all my people. All the blood, all the fear, for your own selfish greed!'

'Bee!' Paul protested. His human fear seemed ludicrous against her madness. At the sound of his voice she flung herself at him with an incoherent howl, and for a moment she grappled with him, and then fell inert at his feet, clutching at her belly and making no sound at all.

Clifford knelt beside her, still not touching her, and Paul dropped to her other side.

'Bee—' Paul said again.

'She doesn't hear you,' Clifford said. 'Let's get her out of here. Put her on the sofa. Then get a doctor.' He took hold of her arm to lift her, and she turned her face up to him. For the strangest second, her face seemed to swim in the uncertain light, and was not hers, but a stranger's, a white, suffering face under tangled dark hair: a face he had never seen before, yet which seemed somehow familiar. She whispered, 'The child.' The impression lasted the least part of a second and was gone—then she was Bee, and hardly conscious.

77

Paul took her other arm, and they lifted her between them and took her, feet dragging, to the drawing-room.

* * *

She recovered very quickly, and at once begged them not to send for the doctor.

'In any case,' she added in a normal voice, 'he won't come out on a Sunday. Doctors don't make calls on a Sunday.'

'They do if it's an emergency.'

'Well it isn't. I'm all right now. Aren't I?' She gazed round appealingly from face to face. 'Aren't I Lulu? Paul? Please. Cliff please don't let him send for a doctor.'

'Bee, I think you need help,' Clifford said gently.

'No! I'm all right. Look, if you send for a doctor, they'll take me away, lock me up somewhere, and I'll never get out. I'm not insane, you know I'm not.'

'Oh Bee, don't be so melodramatic—you won't be locked up. This isn't the Middle Ages.'

'Cliff—Paul—please.' She whispered agonisingly. 'I'm all right now.'

They looked at each other. Eventually Paul said,

'All right, you're okay now, but what if it happens again? You must have help, Bee, you can't go on like this. Look at you—you're skin and bone!'

78

'I'll eat more.'

Clifford laughed.

'Oh Bee—nobody could think you were insane when you say crazy things like that. But truly, you must go and see somebody. We won't force you, but you must promise to go and see someone of your own accord.'

'That sounds like forcing to me,' Bee said bitterly.

'Not necessarily,' Louise put in for the first time. 'They haven't said who you must see. Give them their promise, and you can go and see the dentist, if that's what you want.'

'Louise!' Paul said indignantly.

'Well, don't bully her. Give her another whisky, and let's forget about all this. Give her a chance to get her breath back.'

Oddly enough, Louise's voice carried the day, and they had drinks all round and went to their seats, leaving Bee reclining on the sofa with her eyes half shut, looking white and drained.

'All right,' she said in the end, 'I promise, but you must let me do it in my own time.'

Later, much later, when the others had gone, Paul took Bee onto his lap and sat quietly holding her. He had such a feeling of narrow-escape, as if she had almost died and he had only got her back by a miracle. He held her tightly, and she moved a little in response to his squeeze.

'Bee, were you hallucinating?' he asked at

79

last.

'I don't know. I don't remember.'

'But you were saying some crazy things, just as if you meant them. Who were you thinking of?'

'I don't know, I tell you.'

He was silent a moment longer, and then, 'Bee, why did you tell Clifford I kicked the baby to death?'

As a shock treatment, it produced results. She jerked upright on his lap, and struggled with his hands, trying to unclasp them from round her waist.

'You did!' she cried. 'You murderer, you loathsome violent animal—'

'Bee, I didn't. Bee!—I *didn't.*' He held her on his lap against all her struggles, and at last she subsided and sat still. She turned her head to look at him, and her face was puzzled, like someone trying to understand something intellectually too hard for them.

'No,' she said at last. 'You didn't. That's right, you didn't. And yet—'

'And yet what? What are you thinking about?'

'I can't say it,' she said. 'You did—' uncertainly. 'No, not you. I have the picture in my brain. I have the memory. I can't remember something if it never happened, can I?' She screwed up her face painfully, wrestling with her own mind.

'What is the picture in your memory? Can

80

you tell me?' Paul asked her gently. He was almost holding his breath, afraid of damaging the cobweb of communication that was between them.

'Yes,' she breathed, trying to stare into her memory.

'Tell me. What do you see.'

'You—me. Me pregnant. You hitting me with your fist—fist in my—belly.' She winced. 'Oh! Me, falling, Oh God, on the floor, you—not you—kicking me. Not the child! Not the child! Don't, don't do it!' She cried aloud. Paul soothed her with his hands.

'Not me,' he said.

She didn't speak. She was looking at the dark face, the dark, cruel, hawk-nosed face, brown-skinned. 'Dark,' she said. Paul saw that her pupils were distended, and wondered if this had been a good idea. He tried to shake her gently, to bring her out of it, but her fingers fastened more strongly on his arms as she stared.

'Where is it?' he asked. 'The room. Can you see the room?'

'Yes,' she whispered. Good, she still heard him.

'Describe the room,' he said urgently.

'Yes,' she said again, but more faintly. Then she turned towards him, and he saw her face fill with horror, opening up with terror like a flower petalling outwards; for the room she saw was nowhere she had ever been; nothing

81

like any room she had ever seen. Nowhere in this world, nowhere in this time.

Then she screamed.

CHAPTER SIX

Paul woke late the next morning, so late that he decided to take the day off work. He felt pretty terrible anyway. After the emotional evening he had had a very restless night, wandering in and out of nightmares and dreaming the same short sequences over and over again in the most exhausting way. Bee had been up and down several times too, though she tried not to wake him. Twice she had woken him from a fitful sleep with her crying.

When he finally surfaced at around half past nine, Bee was already up and had gone downstairs. He could hear her moving around, and after a while heard the whistle of the kettle. Tea, he thought. His mouth was like sand after all the whisky they had drunk. He dragged himself up, flung back the covers and went over to the window for a breath of air. It was a still day, more like summer than most of summer had been, with the promise of sunshine and heat later on. The room smelled a bit fusty—probably they had both been sweating a lot in the night. He opened the window right up, and then went back to the bed to turn the covers completely back to air.

And stared. Looked closer. Tiny bloodspots on the sheet, pinprick size. Odd. He shrugged. So much that was odd had happened in the last few weeks. Like those petals. He had caught Bee clearing some up the other day. He didn't know how many more there had been that she had concealed from him. She must be bringing them in from somewhere, not knowing she was doing it. People did some strange things when they were having a nervous breakdown. He must persuade her to go to the doctor. Do it gently.

She was in the kitchen. She was by the sink rinsing out cups, and she looked up as he came in. Her face was exhausted, like somebody at the end of several tethers. Her body in her cotton housecoat was thin and brittle, the flowing grace of her movements quite gone.

'Bad night,' he said, and it was not quite a question.

'Yes,' she said. 'Tea?' They avoided each other's eyes like people who have quarrelled and said unforgiveable things they now regret.

'Please.'

She went across to the stove to fill the pot. He had swept up the iron filings last night before going to bed, and thrown them away. He rather regretted throwing them away— they were a thing you might want to use again. He noticed that she still walked round the pattern, and knowing now of the strength of

83

the magnetic force there, he was rather inclined to agree with her, though how she had known before him he couldn't imagine. Some kind of instinct he supposed. She poured the tea and gave him his cup, and leaned against the sink to drink her own.

'Bee,' he began, and failed to find any tactful way of saying it. 'I think you should go and see a doctor.'

'I'm not mad,' she said sharply.

'All right, you're not, but—'

'But what? What do I tell the doctor? I've come to see you because I remember something that never happened?'

'No, Bee, obviously not but—'

'Well, what then?'

'You're not giving me much chance.' She was silent, sipping her tea and staring resentfully at him over the rim. 'You must admit that you've been behaving rather oddly recently.'

'I don't admit it. How oddly? No more oddly than you. Who's got a fixation about a floor mosaic? Conjuring tricks on Sunday evenings? I haven't done anything strange.'

He thought about the flowers, and then thought that if she was doing it without knowing it, it wouldn't help to mention it now. 'All right,' he said, 'you are behaving perfectly normally. But you've lost weight, you aren't eating properly, or sleeping properly, you *look* ill. You're covered in bruises.'

84

She stared down at her arms in surprise. 'Slight exaggeration. I'm not covered in bruises. There's precisely *one* bruise on my arm. And it isn't *my* fault I'm bruised. I don't do it.'

He was surprised by that. 'What do you mean, it isn't your fault? Nobody's blaming you.'

'They come up in the night.'

'So you bump into things when you're wandering round the house in the dark, that's nothing to be blamed for. But you never used to bump into things. I think your co-ordination is a little out of whack.'

'Oh, that's what you think, is it?'

'Bee, don't be so hostile. I'm worried about you.'

'It's a little late for that. If you'd wanted to worry about me, it should have been years ago. Nothing can help me now.'

'What are you *talking* about—'

'I'm sterile, that's what I'm talking about. Nothing can change that. There's no point in *worrying* about it, dearie,' she said scornfully.

He drank some tea and regarded her thoughtfully.

'Bee, I'm sorry about that. It wasn't my fault—'

'Oh, wasn't it! You're sorry are you? I don't see why—you never wanted a child.'

'All right, then,' he flared up, 'since you want to be brutal, I didn't, I never wanted a child,

85

but—'

'Then you've got what you wanted, haven't you?' she said quietly. He stared, and then said firmly,

'You must go to the doctor. If nothing else, get him to give you some sleeping tablets. Maybe if you got a good night's sleep it would bring back your appetite. I'm tired of seeing you walk about like a sick ghost. If you won't go for anything else, go for that.' He held her stare. 'Please, Bee.'

She sighed and dropped her gaze. 'All right.'

He felt a surge of relief. 'Go today.'

'All right,' irritably. Then, 'I'm sorry I was rude to you.'

He wasn't sure which time she was alluding to, but it seemed churlish to question an apology. 'It's all right, darling,' he said.

'Are you not going to work?'

'Too late now. I'm going to take the day off. Maybe dig the garden for a rest.'

She smiled a little at his attempted joke. 'I'll go to the doctor this morning. He's open until twelve.'

'Do, there's a good girl. It'll take some of the worry off my mind.'

*   *   *

They hadn't intended to meet, but Bee 'phoned him at his office and asked him to be at their usual place at twelve.

'I can't make it by twelve,' he said anxiously. He was afraid his secretary would start to ask questions. Sometimes Louise 'phoned her for a chat. 'It'll have to be twelve-thirty, and even then I might be late.'

'I'll go straight to the flat then, and you can meet me there. Please, Cliff, I have to see you.'

'All right.' He rang off quickly. She didn't sound in any kind of trouble; more the note of wheedling she used to get him to do it again when he was tired or had to get back to the office. Perhaps she'd had a good night's sleep after all, or she'd sorted something out with Paul. She sounded so normal that for a moment he toyed with Louise's idea, expressed the previous night when they got home, that her 'fit' in the kitchen was pure exhibitionism.

'I don't mean to say she necessarily does it on purpose,' Louise had said, cutting off his involuntary protest, 'She may not even know she's doing it. But consciously or subconsciously, she's attention-seeking. I've seen something like it before, when we were at college. She was always doing outrageous things to get people to talk about her.'

'Well, if that's what it is,' Cliff had said, 'she's going a bit too far this time.'

Could it be true? She sounded quite normal now. (Why was she 'phoning from a call-box?) It wasn't acting, what she did last night. Maybe the magnetic vibes affected her—she hadn't been odd before they moved into the new

87

house. But then why wasn't she odd all the time, and why hadn't it started before? No, he was inclined to think it was accumulated strain, after the shock of losing the baby. What she needed was a holiday.

*   *   *

Paul had been digging for an hour and was beginning to feel it was time for a cup of tea. Bee had not long been gone. She said she had an appointment for twelve o'clock, the last appointment of the day. Imagine having to get an appointment to see a doctor! Sometimes they offered you one for a couple of days ahead. As if you would know in advance that you were going to be ill. Can I come and see you next Wednesday, doctor, I'm going to have a bad sore throat?

There was the throbbing roar of a jumbo going past overhead, taking off from nearby Heathrow. He looked up automatically, but couldn't see it anywhere. Say what you will, at least Concorde didn't make as much noise as those buggers: he could almost feel the ground shake. He *could* feel the ground shake, a heavy, muted vibration. 'Go away!' he shouted upwards, and felt better, and then silly.

Cup of tea time. He rammed the fork into the patch of earth he'd just turned and went back to the house, seeing a blackbird hop unhurriedly away in front of him. There was always a blackbird somewhere near when you were digging a garden. In the other house, of course, the blackbird stayed only long enough to see old Footsa sloping up. The one fetched the other. Poor old Footsa. They thought he would love the new house with its bigger garden, but immediately after they moved in he started to mope, and a week later he was gone. Maybe he was pining for his own home. Odd, how he had got out, though. He'd been shut in for the night, since he didn't know the area yet, and when they came down in the morning he'd gone. Still a cat can always get out when it wants to.

He went in at the back door, dragging off his wellies toe to heel just inside, and then went round the corner into the kitchen to put the kettle on. As he went through the door something white fluttered down just out of the corner of his vision and he made a grab at it but lost it. What the devil? He looked up, saw nothing. As he was filling the kettle from the tap, another one floated down. Another of those damn flowers—no, a feather, a small feather, curled—he caught it—no, a flower after all. Damn it, she must stop doing this. He put down the kettle and for no particular reason brushed his hand over the top of his head. They came down like snow, half a dozen of them, from his hair.

He let out an explosive oath, and then leaned forward to stare out of the window down the garden. They must have fallen on his head when he was out there gardening. But from where? There was nothing in the garden that had white flowers. Blown in by the wind from somewhere else? Perhaps. Perhaps. The solution satisfied him for the moment, and he picked up the kettle and turned to cross to the gas stove. And then they started falling again, softly, fluttering round his head and shoulders.

He swore again, and staring upwards, tried to see where they were coming from. There was nothing there, only the plain, white-plastered ceiling, but they were falling from it, steadily as snow, thin, slow, snow. They couldn't. They *couldn't*. They materialised somewhere near the ceiling, and disappeared before they reached the floor. He tried to catch them in his hands, and then began to panic, flailing his arms around, brushing off what couldn't land on him. He brushed madly at his head and shoulders, and his curses thinned and became a whimper.

*   *   *

She had 'phoned Clifford from the first telephone box she could find, but he could not come right away. She would have at least an hour to wait. It was the thing she wanted to avoid. The pressure in her head abated when she talked to other people, abated of course as soon as she left the house but built up again for as long as there was nothing to occupy the humming void between her cranium and jaw. She could not go straight to the bedsit and wait there—she would go round the bend (she found nothing amusing in her own terminology). She would walk around the streets, and if she got desperate, ask someone the way to somewhere. What was that joke, where the American stopped an Englishman in the street and asked him if he knew the way to Park Lane; and when the Englishman said he didn't know, the American said 'Well, you go down here, turn left, then left again—'.

Back to her old stamping ground, her old 'manor'. London is a series of villages, and each Londoner is a village dweller of the most insular and diehard kind. You always go back to your old village, and that's the place you feel most comfortable. Bloomsbury was hers, the British Museum, the college, the university; University College Hospital, Russell Square, Euston Station; Tottenham Court Road, Maples and the little backstreet restaurants between Tottenham Court Road and Broadcasting House. Here she felt safe. Here she felt known. She wandered in through the front gates of University College, unchallenged, though the students were all down and the place was quiet. Still there were students up for resits and special tutorials, and those for summer courses. There was the usual group sitting on the grass of the forecourt, where she herself had sunbathed in Finals term with her cram-books unopened by her side. They had shocked the world by sunbathing in bikinis until the beadles had complained and an edict had been sent out forbidding it.

There were the wide steps and the pillared arch like a grubby version of the old Pearl and Dean advert; and the little side door that led into the Octagon, and the senior common room where she had coffee with her staff friends to the resentment of the older lecturers. Marked out, even then, for a special fate. She had never been able to succeed at anything, and it wasn't because of any lack of ability, but because something in her character or personality or nature or even soul if you would made her a victim, a murderer, a natural sucker. She was a member of other people's fates, not of her own. She was what they had to expiate, she was their guilt, their sin. She belonged to them, and could therefore have no will of her own; or if she did, it *had* to fail, just as the apple had to fall and the stars dance round the universe.

Even Clifford, who had been the fate she was a member of for so long that at times she could not distinguish between herself and him—even to Clifford she was not a person in her own right. He demanded of her, just as they all did. As Paul did, demanding that she play a certain part in the script he had written for himself; so, too, a little more subtly, did Clifford. She was only an extension of his personality. If she showed too much will, it first bored then scared him. He would pack her off if she failed to play her part.

It had got to the stage where she was no longer sure what was her own wish and what theirs. She had acted a part of wanting to order for so long that she did not quite know what, if anything, she wanted on her own behalf. Was it possible for a person to be entirely without personality—well, if not originally it could develop that way. If she took off the bandages, there would be nothing there above her collar.

Her head buzzed. She wanted to kneel down on the steps of the college, there where she had last known who she was, and stop. If only someone would come along with an axe and chop off the non-existent head. Kneel there at the block and die the quick and public way with at least a semblance of identity, having spoken aloud the words of consent to it; perhaps by consenting she could have made the fate her own. She pressed her palms together and looked up at the grimy face of her alma mater, whose bounty could give her nothing but anonymity.

*　　*　　*

It was gone a quarter to one when Clifford reached the bedsitter, and as he ran up the stairs he felt a mixture of excitement and apprehension that was half the charm of these meetings. It was the subconscious longing for discovery and the fear of having one's longings fulfilled that made affairs so much more exciting than marriage. In a sense what he had said about Bee's relationship with Paul could be said about his, Clifford's, with Bee—it could be anyone; for any affair is exciting by its own nature.

He opened the door—it was not locked—and there was Bee, standing near the window, turned half away from him. As he came in she jerked guiltily and thrust her hands behind her like a child caught in the larder.

'Bee?' he said. She backed off from him as he came in—only a mere half-step, but it was redolent of apprehension and guilt. 'What's the matter, darling?' He recognised with a sinking heart that the buoyant, calm mood in which she had telephoned him had gone, to be replaced with the strangeness that was growing stronger each day. Really, he thought, half anxious, half annoyed: 'What is it, Bee?'

She smiled, propitiatingly, and, suddenly apprehensive, he grabbed for her, fought for her hands behind her, and drew them forward. The right was clenched, and he forced it open, to find in it nothing but a pin, an ordinary, dressmaker's pin. The other hand tried to escape gain, and as she shook it to free it, bright drops of blood flew up, spotting his face and shirt.

94

'Bee, what in Christ's name have you been doing?' he cried, and as he spread her hand out, back upwards, he felt slightly sick. With the sharp point of the pin she had evidently been scratching her hand, for there were deep, short, bloody runnels in it, from which the blood seeped bright and rich. The same patter in several places, the same scratch-pattern he had seen on her hip before: as if she had been trying it out, practising. But too deep, deeper than mere scratches. It must have hurt. He stared at her, appalled.

'Bee, why? Why did you do it?'

'I thought I'd show you,' she said, hoarsely. 'I thought I'd show you the face of your own bestiality.' And then, odder than all, she looked down at her hand, trapped in his grip, and her face changed. She shook her head, not a human negative, but in the way an animal shakes the water out of its ears, and a frown of bewilderment and pain came over her face.

'Blood,' she whispered. 'My hand—who?' She looked up at Clifford with tears in her eyes. 'Who did that? Clifford, did you? Why? Why did you do that to me?'

'Oh God,' he said wearily. 'Oh God.' And he drew her into his arms, and held her tightly against his blood-spotted shirt.

* * *

At around four, Louise 'phoned Paul. His

voice as he answered sounded apprehensive, clearing as he recognised Louise's voice.

'What's happened, Lulu?'

'How do you know something's happened?' she delayed long enough to ask.

'Oh, instinct. The sound of your voice. What is it?'

'Well, Cliff just 'phoned me and asked me to get in touch with you. He's with Bee.' For a moment something stung Paul, and he waited for he knew not what words next. 'He says he's taken her to hospital to get her hand dressed— apparently she hurt her hand, and he insisted it was looked at.'

'How did she hurt her hand? What do you mean, hurt?'

'I don't know, Paul—he was a bit vague about that. I have an idea he couldn't say too much where he was—maybe she was listening, I don't know. Anyway, he took her to UCH to get her hand looked at, and while she was there he took the opportunity to speak to a shrink he knows who operates from there, and he's going to try and get to see her before she goes. Cliff says she's a bit shocked, so he may be able to get her kept in overnight, which will give this chap a chance to have a talk to her.'

'Wait, wait, you're going too fast for me,' Paul said. 'How did Clifford happen to be with her when she hurt her hand?'

'I don't know, darling, he didn't say. As I said, he was vague about that bit. You know he

96

works up that way—maybe they were lunching, I don't know.'

'But she was supposed to be going to the doctor at twelve o'clock today. What was she doing up there?'

'I don't know.'

'And what do you mean, she's shocked? What happened? Who's this bloke he's getting to see her? What's he seeing her for?'

'I keep telling you I don't know.'

'You don't know very much, do you Lulu?'

'Well don't take it out on me! I'm only the flippin' messenger, guv.'

'Sorry. Sorry. I'm a bit worried. Where is Cliff now? Perhaps I can speak to him on the 'phone. Maybe the best thing would be to go up there.'

'Yes, perhaps it would.'

'Oh poor Paul, you do sound down. Don't worry darling, I'm sure it's nothing serious, or he would have said. I think it's just an excuse to get her to see someone.'

'That's my business, not his,' Paul said resentfully.

'Well, darling, you don't seem to have been awfully successful so far, do you? After all, we all love Bee and want the best for her. If Cliff can get her to see someone, and it's going to do her good, you shouldn't be cross because it isn't you that did it, should you?'

'No, you're right of course. How sensible you always are, Lulu.'

97

'Well I try to be, my pet. That's what I'm here for. Listen, why don't I toodle over and pick you up in the car and drive you up there? I'm sure you're too upset to make your own way. Then I can hold your hand—metaphorically speaking—through the nasty ordeal.'

Paul laughed aloud. 'Yes, do that, Lulu, that's a very good idea.'

'Right. I'll be with you in fifteen minutes, darling. And *don't worry*.'

'I'll try not to.'

He put down the 'phone and stared bleakly around him. What was happening to his lovely, warm, cosy, stable domestic set-up? What was happening to their lives? Either one or both of them was going crazy, or he was dreaming. He wished it was the latter, for then there'd be some hope of waking up sometime. But he had a horrible feeling that this particular dream had no ending.

CHAPTER SEVEN

'Just talk to him, Bee, that's all. There can't be any harm in that, can there?' Paul said, walking up and down the small hospital room. Bee said nothing, but her eyes followed him as she lay propped on a heap of pillows. Clifford turned away and looked out of the window with its inspiring view of the glazed-tiled wall, grimy frosted windows and drainpipes. Despite what his brain told him, it felt too much like harrying a helpless animal. Intellectually he knew it was for her good; emotionally he wanted to snatch her up and carry her out of here.

'I don't want to,' she said at last. 'That's how they trap you. You've only got to open a book—first they ask you questions, and then they twist the answers and dare you to deny you said it. Then they lock you up and fill you with drugs and cut bits of your brain out.'

'In books, darling, not in real life. You don't think I'd let them do anything to you, do you?'

'Oh no,' she said ironically, and he could hear the drug-slur in her voice, for she had been given tranquillisers. 'You'd do it for my own good. Just as you are now. They'd convince you, and you'd be only too glad to give up the responsibility. That's how they always get you.'

'Darling—!' He stared at her, then turned to Clifford appealingly. 'Cliff, you talk to her.'

He didn't want to get involved, but when he glanced over towards her and saw her tired, harried face, he had to step in.

'Bee, I got you into this, and I'm sorry in a way, but I do think somebody ought to help you. Will you please just talk to this man, and I promise you faithfully that no-one shall do anything to you, nor take you anywhere but home, without your consent.'

'Without my consent?' she said ironically. He knew what she was thinking—first drug me, then my consent can be tricked out of me.

'All right, with or without your consent. No-one shall do anything to you, I promise. You trust me, don't you?'

No, her face said, but 'Yes—all right. I'll talk to him. But it won't do any good. He won't understand.'

'What makes you so sure?' Paul asked her.

'I don't understand myself, and it's my head.'

Outside, in the corridor, Paul said, 'Thanks, Cliff. I don't blame her for being scared. I've been feeling odd myself recently. You don't think it can be catching, do you?'

Clifford looked at him oddly. 'You've been under a lot of strain. It would do you good to have a little while on your own.'

Paul grimaced. 'I don't know that I want to be on my own. You can start to imagine things. Only the other day—' he stopped abruptly. He still wasn't sure of Clifford.

'Yes?' Clifford encouraged him.

'Nothing. Listen, how come she was with you anyway? She was supposed to be going to see her doctor for some sleeping tablets.'

Clifford and Bee had talked about that one. 'She phoned me up, asked if she could talk to me. She wanted to discuss her state of mind with someone.'

'But why you?'

100

Clifford shrugged. 'It can sometimes be easier to talk to someone who isn't involved. You were too close to it all, and Lulu's too close a friend. That's my guess, anyway.' Paul nodded—it seemed reasonable.

'Well, it may have been a blessing in disguise, anyway, this pin business. If she's been hurting herself without knowing it, this may bring it all out into the open and something can be done about it. I only hope—'

'What?'

'That they don't decide she's dangerous and want to lock her up.'

'You would just have to stop them.'

'But I'm not sure how far their powers stretch. Maybe they have the power under law to shut someone up if they're a menace to themselves.'

'Oh don't be so weak! You bloody well stand up for her. Let them take her over your dead body. Where's your fight?'

'I don't feel very full of fight just now,' Paul said tiredly. 'it's been a hell of a week.'

'Why don't you go home with Louise and let her feed you and fill you up with booze, and then have an early night in our spare bed? You'll feel much better for it in the morning.'

'It sounds tempting, but I think I ought to wait and see the doctor.'

'I'll see him tonight,' Clifford said, 'I'll hang on here—you can see him in the morning.'

'Well—'

101

'Go on, man. You can do her much more good by getting yourself into shape, than by hanging round here looking like death warmed up.'

'Suppose she asks for me?'

'You've been watching too many films. She isn't dying, you know.'

'All the same—'

'If she asks for you I'll telephone and Louise can bring you straight over. All right?'

'Oh, all right then.'

'Don't sound too grateful—it might crack your jaw.'

'It's not that I don't appreciate—'

'I was joking. Go on, off with you. I'll hang around while I'm wanted.'

* * *

Peter Cudlipp frowned. 'It doesn't sound too good, does it?'

'Oh, I don't think it's as bad as all that. She only goes cluck from time to time—'

'She would naturally have periods of behaving normally, but that isn't the point. From your account the periods of odd behaviour are growing more frequent, and from superficial damage to herself she's gone to more serious acts. You know where that tends.'

'Oh come—'

'It's a pity she wasn't given help sooner.'

102

'It wasn't a case of giving or not giving,' Clifford said, a little annoyed. 'She's an adult and a strong-minded one. She decided her own fate.'

'There are times when you've got to force someone to accept help, for their own good.'

There they were, those fatal words: for your own good. How right Bee was to foresee it. How often had terrible things been done in that name? Well, he had promised her, and this promise he would keep. Keep faith. He knew nothing of loyalty, and she did not trust him one whit, but this time he would keep his promise. (In the hope, perhaps, that one day someone would do the same by him? A sort of insurance policy, like repenting when death is near.)

'Well, anyway, perhaps you'd just like to talk to her, Peter, and—take it gently, won't you?'

'Don't worry, Cliff,' Peter showed his nice teeth in a professional smile, 'she won't feel a thing.'

*   *   *

He found it useful both physically and psychologically to carry out various small examinations while he was talking. It kept the patient's mind just sufficiently occupied to relax them, and the physical contact was often reassuring. He took her blood pressure, tested her reactions, listened to heart and chest, looked into her ears and eyes, and got her, as gently and quietly as possible, to talk about it.

'I understand you've been bruising yourself quite a lot recently?'

'Not at all,' she said sharply. 'I don't do it to myself—'

'Oh, I meant by accident, of course,' he said soothingly. 'Banging into things by accident. Do you think your balance is affected? Have you had ringing in your ears, a feeling of pressure in the ears and neck?'

She stopped and stared, a little startled. 'Yes,' she admitted reluctantly. 'Sometimes a humming noise and a feeling of tightness—'

'Dizziness? Black specks in front of the eyes?'

'Sometimes,' she said warily.

'Well, that's natural enough in any case,' he said cheerfully, watching her face covertly. 'Your blood pressure is quite a lot down, and that would give rise to similar symptoms.' She looked enormously relieved.

'Blood pressure,' she murmured. He let it sink in.

'I understand you walk in your sleep?'

'So I'm told,' she said. 'I don't remember it when I wake up.'

'Well you wouldn't, would you?' he said smiling. 'That's probably when you get those bruises.' He said it with the air of one successfully accounting for a major scientific puzzle that has been baffling the best brains in the country for months. She nodded slightly. He felt her relax—he was still holding her hand, as if by accident, having just taken her pulse—and added casually, 'But those cuts on your hand were quite another thing. Why did you do that?'

She didn't react for a moment—she frowned as if trying to remember—but as he felt her stiffen with apprehension he changed the question: 'Can you remember what was in your mind when you were doing it? Think back and see if you can get a picture.' Back on your side again, the great detective tracing back a thread.

'Picture—'

'Yes, your husband told me about the other picture in your head, the one you told him about. Perhaps it will help if you can remember what picture was in your head this time. Was it the same, or different?'

'Different,' she replied without thinking. 'He told you that—?'

'He told me everything he thought might help. I want to help, you know,' he smiled coaxingly. 'That's why I'm talking to you—to help.'

'Did he tell you what I'd said about it?'

'What do you mean?'

'It isn't just a picture. It's a memory. I remembered something, but it didn't happen. Could blood pressure affect your memory that way?'

105

'It's possible,' he said. 'Low blood pressure can certainly make you hear and see things. So you actually remember—what?'

'The first one was when I was pregnant. In a strange room. A dark man, dark-skinned—not black, but very brown, as if he was sun-tanned—dark hair, dark eyes.'

'Who is he?'

'Who? He's—I can't think it. Not a name. He's my husband.'

'But not Paul.'

'No, but my husband. I didn't want to marry him,' she burst out, and then stopped, looking puzzled.

'Go on. Why did you marry him?'

'I had to.' That seemed to be all. 'People in my position don't *choose* who to marry.'

'What's he doing in your memory?'

'He's shouting at me. Then he hits me with his fist. I fall down, and he kicks me in the belly, shouting at me all the time.' She shut her eyes in pain. 'He wants to kill the child.'

'Why does he want to do that?'

'It isn't his child.' Tears were beginning to seep out of her closed eyes, and her pulse was growing more rapid. He changed the subject.

'Can you see the room? What does it look like?'

'Plain and bare. White walls painted with colours like jewels. And outside the window, blue sky. It's very hot. It's been hot for weeks. Too hot.'

She opened her eyes abruptly and looked at him. 'You think I'm crazy?'

'No,' he said, matter-of-fact.

'You don't believe in my memory.'

'I believe you remember it. Obviously it didn't happen, but there's a very good reason why this picture is in your mind.'

'What reason?'

'That's what we want to find out, isn't it?' He chafed her hands comfortingly and went on, 'What about the other time? Was there a picture in your mind then?' He deliberately didn't specify which time, hoping she would tell him.

'I knew he was coming in. He had done it to me. I wanted to shock him, make him see how horrible it was.'

'And did it shock him?'

'No. He laughed. That's when I—' Her face grew stiff with fear, her eyes bulging.

'What?' he asked her, pressing her hand urgently. She shook her head. 'What?'

'The pictures are growing,' she whispered. 'All the time. All the time I'm remembering more. I don't want it—I don't want it!'

'Hush, don't think about it. It isn't real,' he soothed her firmly. 'These things didn't happen—you know that. These things are only in your mind, and your mind is making them up to conceal something from you—something in your subconscious mind that you feel guilty about, or ashamed of, or maybe something

107

that was bad and you don't want to remember. Now, if you can discover what that thing in your subconscious is, and deal with it, your mind won't have anything to cover up, and these pictures will go away. Do you understand?'

She was not looking at him, and he couldn't tell if she was listening. Her face was drawn with fear, and her eyes were fixed, glaring over his shoulder. But as he finished speaking he could see that she was thinking about something, and faint expressions flickered over her face as if she was working something out, dealing with various ideas as they arose and putting them aside.

'Bee, do you hear me? Did you understand what I was telling you?'

'Yes,' she whispered at last.

'All right. Now there's nothing to be afraid of,' he went on. 'None of these things ever happened or ever will happen. We must concentrate on finding out what the real thing was. What I suggest is, when you've had a good rest and feel a little stronger, that we arrange for you to see an analyst, and he will help you discover what it is you're hiding from yourself. All you have to do is talk to him, do you understand, Bee?

'Yes,' she whispered again. He talked on for a while until he felt that she was calm, and then left her to see the nursing staff and make sure she was given enough tranquillisers to give her a good night's sleep. After speaking a few words to him in the corridor, Clifford came back in to see her.

'Bee?' he whispered, tiptoeing across to the bed where she lay with her eyes shut. He thought she might already be asleep, but she opened her eyes and looked at him with such an expression of—resignation?—hopelessness?—that his heart ached for her.

'What is it?' he whispered.

'He didn't understand,' Bee said. 'But I think I do.' She closed her eyes again against the tears and said, 'Clifford, I want to go home.'

* * *

Peter Cudlipp faced the two men across his desk, and knew before he started that he was not going to carry the day.

'I feel most strongly that, for her own safety, she should not be allowed to go home. She already has a long history of self-inflicted wounding, and although these wounds are at the moment very slight, there is no doubt at all in my mind that they will develop into something more serious. She is very much imbalanced at the moment.' He watched the stubborn expression solidify on the husband's face. 'I recommend in the strongest terms that she be admitted to hospital, to a place where not only can she be given the proper treatment, but also be adequately protected from hurting herself—or anyone else.'

Clifford looked sidelong at Paul. Already he was feeling that Peter was right and that, despite his promise, Bee ought to be taken to hospital; but Paul was evidently going to be stronger—or was it more stupid?

'I'm sorry, doctor, but she wants to go home and I'm going to take her.'

'You understand that this is against my recommendation *and* that of my colleague whom I have consulted in this case? And that very serious consequences may result?'

'I understand, and I'm willing to take that risk, but I don't think anything will happen.'

'Well, I can't force you to admit her,' Peter said with a slight shrug, 'but I do want to impress upon you that she should be watched all the time. And you should take care to keep sharp objects like knives away from her. She'd be much better, you know, in a hospital for a few weeks,' he made one final plea.

'I'm sorry—' Paul said.

'I hope you don't have cause to be,' Peter interrupted him. 'Well, about her mental condition: I think the initial problem *was* the miscarriage,and her condition arises from the shock of that occurrence. She feels some kind of guilt in that connection—she may have convinced herself that it was some act of her own which caused the miscarriage—it does happen sometimes—and she is subconsciously trying to rid herself of that guilt by making up these stories in which someone else is to blame.'

'A sort of schizophrenia?' Clifford suggested.

'Schizophrenia often takes that form in order to disassociate the subject from guilt,' he agreed.

'So what can we do to help her?' Paul asked.

'Other than by taking my advice? Well, what she needs is to face up to whatever it is she feels guilty about. But I don't feel that there's anything you can do in that respect. She needs to see a trained psychiatrist.'

'Perhaps I can persuade her to see one of her own accord,' Paul said.

'At the very least, I recommend you do everything in your power to so persuade her.'

*   *   *

'Thank you, Paul,' Bee said once they were in the car. 'I didn't think you'd do it.'

'It's all right, darling. I understand a lot more now than I did,' Paul said, holding her hand. They exchanged a long, curious look. 'It'll be all right.'

'I don't think so,' she said in a low voice. 'But I must go home.'

'A complete rest, a holiday, that's what you need,' Louise said from the front seat. 'A few weeks basking about on golden beaches in the S. of F. with a bottle of white wine and a bag of peaches at your side.'

'Sounds inviting,' Bee said, trying to laugh.

'And some bronzed young god paying you outrageous compliments,' Louise went on.

'You sound too convincing, Lulu,' Clifford said, his eyes on the driving mirror. 'Are you sure this isn't what you're recommending for yourself?'

'Could be, Cliff, I wouldn't mind if I could get you to play.'

'Play or pay?' Paul put in.

'Both, if I know Lulu,' Cliff said. It was a good attempt at sounding like old times. Bee sat in the back seat like a ghost of herself. In her handbag was the bottle of sleeping tablets which might represent the last resort, a sort of comfort, except that she felt too much in the grip of what was happening to her to be sure she would have the will to do it—however bad things got. She didn't know for sure if she were going mad, or if she were sane and everything else was going mad, but which ever way it was, she was the focus, the chosen victim; as she always had been.

By request, Clifford let them out at the end of the road and then drove away, leaving Paul to support Bee's hesitant steps back to the house.

'Home, Bee,' he said as they reached the front gate. The handsome old house with its friendly face waited for them, squatting at the end of the path like the pagan god who owned

112

their lives. It was as if they had rebelled against their fate for a little, but had now come back to be done with as the god wished, knowing that however bad it was to belong to him, it was worse to belong to no-one. I submit me, and if not in love, at least in understanding.

'Yes,' she said. 'I'm glad you didn't let them take me away.'

'I couldn't have let them do that,' he said, fitting his key into the lock, and turning it. He pushed open the door very slowly, and they stepped into the hall, listening, apprehensive. The house was silent—not even the ticking of a clock—and still. The utter stillness seemed to accept them back. Bee released herself from Paul's encircling arm and walked forward strongly, and Paul shut the front door to complete their privacy.

CHAPTER EIGHT

The further from the house he went, the greater was the sensation of relief, of a weight lifted. It was like a flight--at least emotionally, for intellectually he knew it was only a respite. Even if he had the choice, he could not have left the thing unfinished—and he had no choice. At the end of the day he must go home to Bee; she was, if not his responsibility, at least his fate.

But for the time being, there was a respite.

Clifford had arranged it, saying that Paul needed a little time to himself; a good friend, Clifford. He had arranged for Louise to take Bee shopping in the West End, with lunch out somewhere, and in the evening, since Louise had a constituency meeting to attend, Clifford was going to entertain Bee at his house. It was all arranged. Paul would pick her up there when he came home.

But for the moment he was fleeing westwards into Wiltshire. It was a cold, bright day, the sky the pale, milky blue of an old man's eyes. The world was still green, but here in the West Country the trees were already bare, stripped of their inessentials for the winter, waiting for the dust-sheets of snow to cover them. The sun was a dull-gold coin, slightly fuzzed at the edges, wandering in an unfocussed way as the road switched direction. All men go westwards with the sun, he thought; like the tide; drawn by the promise of greenness in the west.

Paul was being drawn by the promise of another maze. It was in the grounds of an old manor-house near Salisbury, and was open to the public until the end of October, and Clifford suggesting he needed to get away by himself was an ideal opportunity to fit in a visit. He had read about it in one of his library books, and he hoped he might learn something, without having any idea of what he wanted to learn.

It served, at least, to keep his mind from time to time away from Bee. Had he been right to bring her home? There was no more hysteria, no more nervous startling; she seemed calm, almost normal; but there was something about her that troubled him, some quality he could hardly put a name to, a kind of doomed brightness, an unnatural light like that of a storm sun. No, that was fanciful. He shook his head. It was enough for one of them to have fantastic imaginings. He must hold hard to reality if he was going to be able to help her. Yet he wished she was less—what? Resigned? Yes, perhaps that was it. She was *too* quiet. It worried him.

*   *   *

The manor house stood alone outside a village in a sea of ploughed fields. Paul pulled his car up onto the grass verge off the road and walked to the open white gate where he was met by the caretaker, who greeted him like a man in sore need of company.

'Don't get many visitors this late in the season,' he said. 'Come to see the maze, have you?'

'That's right,' Paul said. 'You must be nearly ready to close up.'

'End of the month. This way—I should keep to the duck-boards if I was you. We've had a lot of rain, and that path's in a bad way. A load

115

of gravel wouldn't do that path any harm at all. Have to think about it next year, if we're going to get another season like this one.'

'A lot of rain?' Paul hazarded.

'Lots of visitors,' the caretaker corrected. 'Never seen the like! Hundreds. We had more in one month this year than we've had in a whole season some years.'

'Why the sudden interest?'

'Dunno.' He shrugged. 'Of course,' he added, looking sideways at Paul, 'it's a very fine example of its type, well worth seeing. Seems they go to Stonehenge, then fit this in on the way back. Americans, Germans and Japanese. And this year, Arabs.'

'Really?'

'Scores of 'em. Can never tell what they're thinking, though. Japanese, I've got used to them. Ask questions, they do, nonstop. Facts, that's what they want, facts and figures and dates. But Arabs—I don't know what they come here for. They look at it and go away—don't seem to show any interest.'

'Maybe they're thinking of buying it,' Paul joked, and was sorry. The caretaker looked offended.

'You can't buy a thing like this. Prehistory, this is.' In silence they walked down the muddy path between neatly clipped hedges of evergreen, through another gate and across a closely mowed meadow and suddenly the maze was in front of them.

116

'There,' the caretaker said. 'What do you think of that?'

It covered an area of perhaps twenty-five feet square; its size alone at first stunned Paul. The grass of it was old and dark, almost black, the chalky paths standing out lividly against the ancient turf, comfortably broad enough to walk along. It seemed sunk a little into the ground, a wound in the earth's face. It was so ancient, it made him shiver.

The caretaker watched his face askance, and seemed pleased at his reaction.

'Gets you, the first time, doesn't it?' Paul nodded. 'I've been here over twenty years, but when I'm on my own, I still feel funny about it sometimes. Like there's something crawling up my back. Mind you, that could be the static. Chockfull of static, this place is. I've seen a dog's hair stand on end with it as far off as the gate.'

Paul scarcely heard him. With his eye he traced the lines of the path. The windings were not identical to those of his own maze, but the effect was the same—the path working in and then out—and the overall shape, what Louise had called brain-shaped, it was the same.

It was so old, it was awesome, but, almost in spite of himself, Paul was compelled to go forward, to put his foot on the path with the intention of walking the maze. He withdrew it, however, with a sharp jerk as a mild electric shock rapped at the base of his neck. The

117

caretaker nodded approvingly.

'Give you a buzz, did it? Told you it was full of static. Some people don't feel it, but some tell me it like tickles their feet as they walk round. Of course, it gets worse this time of year.'

'Why?' Paul asked.

'After the summer. It like builds up all through the summer. Like thunder storms— you always get a lot of them at the end of summer. They say its the same at Stonehenge. You been to Stonehenge?'

'No, I'm rather ashamed to say I haven't.'

'Going there afterwards?'

'No, I only came to see this.'

'Got some special interest, have you?'

'Yes.' Paul did not particularly want to bring it all out. Unable to bring himself to put his foot on the path again, he began to walk round the outside of it, and the caretaker followed him. Was it auto-suggestion, or did the ground under his feet 'buzz'? Like a very high-frequency vibration. He could almost hear it, through the soles of his feet, up his spine, to his ears, a pressure, a high-pitched humming like a distant dynamo. He felt his hairs lifting. His eyes wandered round the paths and the buzzing in his head increased, blackness swam in, he felt himself falling . . .

'Steady! You almost went then! Here, come back a bit, and have a sit down—the old static's very bad today. You went dizzy, didn't you?'

Paul allowed the caretaker to guide him away, but he had soon recovered himself, and felt a little ashamed at his weakness. He thought he had better be going. The place oppressed him with its brooding silence. He asked if there was a guide book he could buy.

'No, we haven't got one,' the caretaker said sadly. 'Reason being that no-one really knows anything about the maze. It's always been here, and that's as much as we know. But I tell you what, if you're really interested, and you've got a bit of time to spare, you ought to go and have a word with Mr Masters.'

'Who's Mr Masters?'

'He's an old boy lives in the village. Retired. He lives in Keys Cottage with his dogs and he never goes out much, so you'd be bound to find him in. Now he's made a lifetime study of these mazes all over the world, and if anyone knows anything about them, it's him.'

'In the village, you say?'

'That's right. It's the white cottage right next to the George and Dragon—you can't miss it. He'd be tickled pink if you was to pay him a visit. He loves talking about mazes—his pet subject. Straight down the road here, into the village, and it's on the right. He can't get about much, so he could do with the company.'

* * *

Paul's knock was so long unanswered that he

almost went away. When the door was opened it revealed a man so bent and old that Paul's heart sank. It did not seem possible that anything useful could be learnt from this shrunk and simian creature, shabbily clothed, holes in the elbows of his shapeless cardigan, tobacco ash liberally covering his front. A few shreds of white hair were combed carefully across the top of a head as innocently pink as a baby's. Unexpectedly dark eyes looked up at Paul with an almost plaintive wonder.

'Mr Masters?' Paul asked hopelessly. 'I was recommended to come to see you about mazes.'

'Mazes? Yes, good, of course. You've come to the right place. Do come in, Mr—?'

'Hague.'

'Mr Hague. Do come in. I'm sorry I was so long answering the door, but, as you see, I find it difficult to move with any speed. In fact the door was open. The village people let themselves in, but you wouldn't know that, of course. Have you come far?'

'From London.' Paul followed him as he crept with painful slowness into the back parlour, which was cluttered with furniture and books and sagging cushions and hot from a large log fire. A shapeless hairy balloon on the floor before the fire stirred as they entered, and Mr Masters said, 'Don't mind Sophy, my bitch. She won't hurt you. She's blind, poor creature. She's actually older than me in her

120

own terms, but she still seems to enjoy her food and she's company for me, so I hesitate to have her put away. I wonder sometimes if we have the right to determine such things, although of course we determine them the other way by interfering with our medicine and veterinary know-how to *stop* them dying, so I suppose one must accept the responsibility one has created. I hope you don't think it too early for a little something? Can I offer you a glass of sherry? Or would you prefer whisky? I think I have some whisky left.'

'Sherry would be excellent, thank you,' Paul said, and managed to stop himself offering to pour them the drinks. He felt ashamed of his earlier thoughts. The old man crept across the room to the sideboard and once there managed the glasses and decanter briskly. Paul collected his full glass, and forced himself to wait patiently while Mr Masters worked his painful way back to his chair by the fire. Then Paul sat, tasted his sherry, found it excellent, and said so.

'Thank you,' Mr Masters said. 'It comes, like yourself, from London. I have a dozen a year sent down—my one little indulgence of the flesh. Life without a decent sherry would be intolerable. I caught the habit at Oxford before the war, and I've never been able to break it. The first war, I meant, of course. Before the second war I believe the fad was for gin-cocktails.' He smiled, sending fan-like ripples of creases outwards from both eyes and lips. 'Nowadays I expect it would be "pot", at the very least. So you have come from London? That argues a very strong interest in mazes. May I ask what prompts it?'

'I have one,' Paul said. Masters straightened perceptibly in his chair, and listened with an air of suppressed excitement as Paul told him about the finding of the maze, and its appearance. Masters asked him one or two questions, and then leaned back in his chair with a sigh.

'How very fortunate you are,' he said. 'It is the most exciting find to have made, and were it not that I am hardly able to get to the front door and back, I would certainly like above all things to come and see it. From what you say I think it cannot be one of the originals, but the building of them went on for a very long time, and it is likely that it is built upon an authentic site. Now, my dear sir, what was it you wanted to know?'

'Anything you can tell me. I know nothing at all about mazes, other than that they are supposed to have something to do with the earth's magnetic fields.'

Mr Masters sipped his sherry slowly and looked into the fire.

'I will tell you what I know, and what I think,' he said, 'but it is possible you may think me no more than a crank. It depends a lot on how you have been educated. Some educations

122

include things which other educations scorn. In the old days, of course, one had a fair idea of how much any particular person knew, but nowadays one can never be sure. One comes across the most startling gaps, alongside mines of knowledge even more startling.' He turned his eyes towards Paul and said firmly, 'I believe the mazes to be artefacts of the Atlanteans, either of colonists or of survivors. It is difficult to be sure on that point, since we do not have any definite dates to go on.'

'Atlanteans?' Paul asked doubtfully. 'But I thought Atlantis was a myth?' He felt a sinking of heart. The old man was going to turn out to be a crank after all.

'Many things that we think of as myths are in reality race-memories of actual occurrences. We know comparatively little about Atlantis, but on the other hand we know it existed, where it was, and that it was destroyed in or around the year 9850BC. It was destroyed by some kind of cataclysm which affected very clearly defined portions of the globe. The Flood talked of in the Bible was part of that cataclysm. There are also some people who think it was that cataclysm which altered the earth's axis, but I have my own reasons for doubting that.'

'But why do you think the mazes were built by the Atlanteans?' Paul asked, clinging to the main point.

'For two reasons,' Mr Masters said. He

123

raised two fingers the better to count them off. He was clearly enjoying himself. 'Firstly, their age. The oldest of them is at least that old, more likely older, and we do not know of any other civilisation of that period advanced enough to have made them. Secondly, we do know that the Atlanteans made use of electric power. Obviously they cannot have created their electricity by the use of fossil fuels. That leaves the possibilities that they powered they dynamos with some kind of natural energy, solar-power, or wave-power or something of that sort; or that they tapped the huge store of the earth's electricity. My belief is that they did both.'

'And the mazes? What would that make them?'

'There I am afraid I'm a little hazy. They are built only at places where lines of magnetic force meet, and that is obviously significant. One possibility is that they mark the sites where the power-houses were built, or at least where the machines were sited. The objection to that is that there are no archaeological evidences of any kind of associated artefacts. Another possibility is that the mazes are themselves power-houses, that they focussed and perhaps directed the electrical power, rather in the way that a wireless transmitter focusses radio waves.'

'But if that were the case—?' Paul began, frowning. Mr Masters anticipated him.

'Why can't we still use them? Because, of course, we don't have the necessary receivers. You can't listen to the wireless unless you have a set.'

Paul thought about it for a moment. 'The caretaker at the maze here said that the area is very full of static electricity.'

Mr Masters nodded. 'That may, of course, be coincidence, but I think not. If either of my theories were correct, the maze would be sited on a place where that would be the case. But the mazes may be sited in that way for quite a different reason.'

'And what is that?' Paul asked.

'I don't know. I mean, that the mazes may have had a quite different purpose, which made the presence of the magnetic and electrical fields necessary. Folk-lore tells us that the Atlanteans were skilled in magic. But any manipulation of energy would seem like magic to those who didn't understand it. Whatever their "magic" was, I feel very strongly that the mazes were essential to it, and that the shape of the maze is significant.'

'A friend of mine thought the shape was like a brain.'

Masters nodded. 'Yes. It is. Other people have said it is shaped like the "mushroom" cloud of an atomic explosion. That, of course, is our present-day magic. With one wave of the hand we can make whole cities disappear. I wonder what our primitive ancestors would

125

have made of that little conjuring-trick?'

After a short silence, Paul took up the point again. 'But supposing the maze is brain-shaped, how would that be significant? I mean, what do you think the magic could have been that would demand that shape?'

Mr Masters spread his hands ruefully. 'I wish I were able to supply the answers as ably as you provide the questions. All I can do is offer you ideas to play with. I don't *know* anything.' He looked at Paul as if gauging his intelligence, or perhaps receptiveness.

'Go on,' Paul encouraged him. 'I'm happy to have even your ideas.'

'Well, then, we know that man once had a great many physical attributes that he no longer has, which he has lost through civilisation just as he has lost his tail, and his thick coat of hair. We know this both from study of remains, and from study of the few primitive races who still live on this planet. We can also surmise a great deal from the vestiges of primitive reactions in civilised man. We know, for instance, that man used to be able to prick his ears as animals do, and some people are still able to move their ears slightly, although the muscle has atrophied through disuse. Man used to have a much more acute sense of smell, and some people can still smell things that are not perceptible to others.' Paul nodded in appreciation of the point.

'We can surmise also,' Mr Masters went on,

'that at one time the species used to produce a sexual smell to stimulate mating, as the more primitive primates do. And so on. I won't bore you with a list of our lost abilities. You will be able to supply them yourself. Now, I have often wondered whether, along with these physical attributes we have lost, we might not have lost some mental attributes. Dolphins, for instance, have ways of communicating with each other which are beyond our understanding, which do not, apparently, involve the use of acoustics at all. Might not the appearance of a vestigial mental power, which the Americans call ESP, be an indication of mental powers which we once had but have lost through disuse; powers which we would nowadays class as magic, since we do not understand them?'

Paul fidgeted a little at this new turn the conversation was taking. 'But surely,' he said, 'human telepathy is just a myth. Our brains simply aren't built for it.'

'Precisely,' said Mr Masters. 'They aren't built for it, any more than our ears are built to swivel about as they once did.'

'But we lost that power gradually, through evolution. Evolution takes a very long time.'

'Ten thousand years is a long time. Who can say how long it takes to lose a mental power? Some evolutionary changes have taken place in as little as several hundred years. Moreover, the break in this flow of evolution caused by a cataclysm of the order that destroyed Atlantis might have an incalculable effect on the natural order of things. And again, it could well be that the Atlanteans have developed this power to a higher degree during their twenty-thousand year civilisation than the primitive races outside the island. This would mean that when they were destroyed, most of those with the power were destroyed.'

'You make it all sound very plausible,' Paul said unwillingly. Mr Masters leaned forward a little.

'My dear sir, I don't wish to persuade you of anything. I myself have to admit that I don't know anything at all. All I wish to do is lay before you some possibilities which cannot be entirely discounted. *If* the Atlanteans had some mental power which we ourselves have lost, and *if* the mazes were in some way useful, perhaps in the magnifying or transmitting of that power, then it might be that the shape is significant, perhaps only in a symbolic or decorational way, but significant none the less.'

There was much to be thought over in what Mr Masters had said, but one way or another Paul did not feel he had gone very far along the road to discovery. It was time, however, to be making his move. Mr Masters tried to press him to stay for another glass of sherry, but Paul made his excuses.

'Let me at least recommend to you some

books on the subject which are not wholly uninteresting,' he said. Paul produced a pen and the back of an envelope and the old man wrote carefully and in legible script the titles and authors of some half-dozen works.

'I must warn you that they are not all sound on the subject. I'm afraid Atlantean cranks tend to be unselective, but I'm sure in reading them you will be able to filter out what is wholly absurd, without rejecting what is worth considering.'

Paul received the envelope and pen again, and made his way to the front door. Mr Masters civilly accompanied him, and on the doorstep Paul shook hands and thanked the old man for his conversation and hospitality.

'Not at all, not at all,' Mr Masters said. 'I am very pleased to have met you. I welcome visitors, house-bound as I am. Any time you are passing this way, any time at all, I shall be delighted to see you. I hope you will remember to call.' It was said almost wistfully, and Paul hurriedly reassured him. He turned to go, and, finding the pen and envelope still in his hand, he turned back on an impulse.

'What would you make of this, sir?' he asked. Hurriedly he scribbled the four-line pattern of the scratches on Bee's hands and arms and passed it over to Mr Masters. The latter glanced at it, and passed it back in a matter-of-fact way.

'I would say it was the trident, the trident

sign of Poseidon, the sea-god, supposedly the chief deity of Atlantis. Why do you ask?'

'Oh, nothing, no reason at all,' Paul said. He thrust the envelope into his pocket, took his leave again, and hurried to his car. As he drove away, Mr Masters was still at the cottage door, watching him go.

CHAPTER NINE

Louise came in from helping with the washing-up and found Clifford and Paul silent in the drawing-room, engrossed in a book.

'How sociable you are!' she exclaimed. 'If we'd known you had nothing to say to each other we would have left *you* to do the washing-up.'

'Where's Bee?' Paul asked automatically.

'Oh she's all right. She's just making some more coffee. Says she's got a raging thirst. I'm a bit thirsty too.'

'Must be all the talking you've been doing.'

'Must be the ham,' she corrected him with dignity. 'I say, she's much better, isn't she? You were right after all, Paul, not to send her away. Obviously just coming home was a medicine to her.'

'Yes,' Paul said, but there was a hint of doubt in his voice which Clifford noticed. Catching his questioning eye Paul went on,

130

'She's certainly much calmer, and I think she sleeps better.'

She's entered a new phase, Clifford thought, without knowing quite why he thought it. Both of them could have told of another development, the silent savagery that had crept into her lovemaking; but naturally they did not mention that. To Clifford it was only an intensification of the passion she had always shown, but to Paul it was something entirely new. She had always more or less submitted, though with excellent grace, to his attentions. Now she responded with a passion beyond his wildest dreams, but it still did not make him happy. Still it ended in weeping for her, and still he could not be sure if she really felt anything for him at all. It seemed more as if she were clinging to some act of which she understood the purpose: something to tie her more firmly to a world from which she was becoming increasingly more distant.

'On the other hand,' Clifford prompted him.

'On the other hand? I don't know. I can't put a name to it.' They fell silent at the sound of Bee's footsteps coming down from the kitchen, and in a moment she entered with the tray of coffee, pausing on the threshold to look round sharply for a second before coming in. In the old days she would have said something like 'Talking about me?' in a gay tone. Now she said nothing. Louise picked up the conversation for them all.

131

'Well, what were you two reading with such deep concentration when I came in? You won't believe it, Bee, but they were both nose-in-book, miles away, when I came in. Not a word to say to each other.'

'I believe it,' Bee said. 'Especially Paul.'

'What is it this time, anyway? Still mazes?'

'Sort of—an extension of the subject, anyway,' Paul said, holding out his book to Louise, spine foremost, for her to see.

She read it, moving her lips, and then looked up with a query. 'Atlantis?' she said. 'What's that got to do with mazes?' Without waiting for an answer she looked at Clifford's book and raised the second eyebrow to join the first. 'It's all nonsense anyway, isn't it? Fairy tales?'

'Scoffer.' Bee chided her amusedly.

'Not a fairy tale at all,' Paul said robustly. 'It's been proved beyond a doubt that the place existed, that it was civilised, and that it was destroyed by a natural calamity nine-thousand-odd years B.C.' Louise did not look convinced.

'That'll teach you to try and alter the ignorance of a lifetime,' Bee smiled. 'Coffee anyone? Clifford?'

'Thanks. This is very interesting, anyway, even if I do have to take it with a handful of salt.'

'You aren't meant to believe everything as gospel,' Paul said, slightly nettled. 'It merely proposes some reasonable explanation for

132

some actual phenomena.'

'But what,' Louise said with underlined patience, 'has it got to do with mazes?'

'Perhaps nothing. It was simply another step along the detective's trail,' Paul said.

'Defective's trail, more like,' Louise said sweetly.

'Oh, I shan't tell you then,' Paul said.

'No, go on. I'd like to hear it.'

'Give it to her both barrels,' Clifford said. Paul looked from face to face, trying to gauge the strength of the general scepticism, and then said,

'Oh, all right. I told you before that no-one knows what the mazes were for. Well, somebody—not anyone terribly well established in the scientific field—'

'In other words, a crank,' Clifford translated.

'As you will,' Paul said with dignity. 'Anyway, someone suggested that they might have been built by the Atlanteans. They are around the right date, archaeologically, and the Atlanteans are supposed to have been great guns on electricity and magnetism, so that would fit in.'

'How civilised were these people supposed to be?' Louise asked.

'That again is so much guesswork. Reports seem to conflict. On the one hand they had a very sophisticated knowledge of astronomy, engineering, architecture, a complex

133

vocabulary and the first ever phonetic writing-system. They knew all about irrigation and intensive farming, had complex canal systems, and some people even say they had aircraft. On the other hand, there was supposed to be an element amongst them that studied black magic and believed in all sorts of pagan gods.'

'In fact, that was what was supposed to have brought about the end—playing around with black magic, wasn't it?' Clifford said.

'Oh yes, if you believe in the retributive idea of the cataclysm. But it was said that there was an element that had gone to the bad and worshipped the devil, did sort of Frankenstein tricks of trying to create human life, and even performed human sacrifices. But I don't know about that.'

'It sounds to me the merest lot of bunkum,' Louise said. 'If you ask me, Paul, your interest in this mosaic of yours has led you down a back alley. Why don't you stick to facts? The magnetism bit is fact—we've all seen that. But all this stuff about Atlantis and devil-worship—'

'I *said* I didn't go along with that bit,' Paul said crossly. Louise waved a hand dismissively. 'Besides, whatever else you like to pooh-pooh, the cataclysm *was* fact.'

'Nonsense. There's no written record of it.'

'Because the only people who could write then were the Atlanteans and they were destroyed in the flood.'

134

'Very convenient,' Louise said derisively.

'There are other ways of recording things than simply writing,' Clifford put in. 'Race memory makes the cataclysm as near fact as anything we can find. We even know the date it happened—the night of October the thirty-first—Halloween or, Hollow E'en. "Hollow" means "dead" of course. That's why November the first was called All Souls' day—in memory of the nation that died.'

'How did you know that?' Paul asked.

'I'm an educated man,' Clifford smiled.

'You're wrong there, anyhow,' said Louise, 'because November the first is All Saints', not All Souls'.'

'I said it *was* All Souls'. The Christian church didn't like the pagan worship so they took over the feast and called it All Saints'. But people continued to put out the milk and food on Hollow E'en, and to light candles in their windows, so the Church gave in and made November the second All Souls'.' This bit of confident chat successfully silenced Louise, for a moment, but she came back to the attack undismayed by saying.

'All right, be that as it may, you have no proof or even evidence that the mazes were anything to do with the Atlanteans.'

'No,' Paul said. 'We don't know anything about the mazes at all: that's why it's so fascinating to speculate.' All this time Bee had not spoken, and Paul now glanced at her

135

sideways—most of his glances at her nowadays were covert; they lived together always with a gap left between them, holding apart like two chapped surfaces, because to touch would be too painful. She was sitting on the edge of the sofa, not sprawled or tucked up as she would have been in former days. Her hands were folded round her cup as if she were trying to warm them, and she was staring at the ground fixedly. He doubted if she had heard anything of what had passed.

There had been times when he had felt he had been right not to let her be admitted to hospital; but there were also times, increasingly more times, when he felt that it was not what would have been best for her. Yet he felt that he had had no choice. Whatever happened now, it had been forced upon him by the weight of circumstance that was building up like water against a dyke. When the dyke burst and the water flooded in, all would be made clear. Then, of course, it would be too late to do anything more than say 'Oh, that was it, was it?' Cold comfort.

* * *

That night Paul would not have made love to her, for when he gathered her bones into his arms his pity outweighed his love, and he wanted only to weep for her. But she needed more than that from him. Now, after all the

136

months of holding herself back from him, body arched like a cat's with distaste, she pressed against him. She would not let him turn off the light. Every night she was afraid that there would be no more light, that the morning would not come again and she would be left to wander in an eternal darkness filled with inexpressible horror: she clung to him as to the last rays of the setting sun, for he was the symbol and the remnant of her past life. Her marriage to him, though it had been the denial of all she would, in youth, have hoped for and expected of herself, was at least a part of the real world, of departing sanity. Its very ordinariness had been reassuring, when she had still been capable of receiving comfort.

Now she held on to him like a lifeline, and with a fierce physical passion that had nothing to do with love and little to do with him, she ran her hands over him, butting at him with her hips, guiding his penis into her with a kind of desperate, greedy haste. She made a sound like pain when he entered her, but held him to her all the same, gripping him as if she were hanging over a precipice. Unwilling as he was, his lust was aroused by her—the excitement of rape, almost—and he moved with increasing haste and helplessness until he came, both of them speaking aloud in the tongues of beasts. And now it was not only she who wept, afterwards. He wept because he had never known her, and she was going from him.

He fell asleep almost at once, cradled in her arms, his head in the hollow of her shoulder. Bee lay awake, feeling her tears drying on her cheeks and his wet on her neck, feeling the little eddy of life made by their movements dying down into the stillness of the house; waiting for the sound to begin, the humming sound that came up from a depth beyond hearing as gradually as the movement of the clock's hand so that it was impossible to tell at what point it was first audible.

Inside her skull her brain, her mind hung separate and ripe like a fruit only just attached by the frailest of stems: a mind no longer in her control, a mind taken over, belonging outside but still sentient, just as her self had belonged to another's fate but still had felt her pain. Her memories grew, memories of what had never happened, memories as perfectly detailed, as sure, as coloured and etched as immutable as her memories of her own life. She *had* done these things, seen, heard, felt, lived them, though they had not happened; each day a little more remembered, a little more added, extending the story, filling in the gaps, as senseless, inconsequential, as fatal as real life, tending towards what end?

What do you want of me? she asked into the silence. She was theirs and would do whatever it was all unknowing, going without knowledge or consent to her fate like the calf to the altar and the cold gleam of the priest's knife: unconsenting, that the gods might be kind.

Sacrifice. A life offered for a benison, a life to stand before the gods, its bowed head to take the punishment and avert the evil, its blood to wash the altar-stone of the priests' iniquities, its blood for the people, for the new life, for the corn. Sacrifice to avert the supreme terror, the end of life, the eternal darkness; one death, but not the death of my people. The tears flowed, and still she said I do not understand, I do not consent. The tears ran down her face unimpeded and soaked into his hair, matting it like blood, though he slept all unknowing. He did not wake even when she got up and left him, only stirred and grunted a little, feeling out and stretching a little in the unexpected space.

*   *   *

Paul woke to clamour and panic, threshing to release himself from the clouds of unconsciousness that fogged his thinking, crying out incoherently until gradually the night and the house solidified round him and he could be aware that he was alone in the bed, and that the quiet hummed with that muted vibration. He sat up, rubbing his face to bring back the feeling of being awake. 'Bee?' he said tentatively. That sound—the 'fridge? Too loud. Things sound louder in the night—the click of a light switch sounds like the walls cracking open. But too loud, still; Christ, he could feel the bed shaking.

'Bee?' he said again. She must have gone downstairs. She was wandering in her sleep again. He swung his feet over the side of the bed and stood up, and fear ambushed him from the corners of the dark room. Something was happening. The old primitive reaction took over. The hair on his scalp raised itself to make him look larger and more frightening to an enemy; his heart beat faster to send the blood round to his muscles more quickly; his skin prickled as the surface blood vessels closed themselves off to minimise blood-loss from any possible wounds.

All this happened without Paul's knowledge or will: he merely felt the shiver of fear, and began to walk, raising himself involuntarily on tiptoe, towards the stairs. Descending the stairs was like descending into the belly of a ship, going down the tiers towards the engine-room. The humming noise grew louder, and he seemed to step down into it as palpably as into water, ankle deep, waist deep, chest deep, until it closed over his head and the humming, vibrating noise that filled the house seemed to be inside his head instead of around it.

There was light, too, light enough to see by, though without any apparent source: it was all around, like the sound. Quite distinctly, Paul thought I'm dreaming this; and knew by the quality of the thought that he was not. He was living it. At the foot of the stairs he turned towards the back of the house, heading without needing directions for the kitchen, and the humming and the light intensified as if with a note of triumph. His steps were leaden, he seemed to have to force his way through this light/sound atmosphere that held him back like a weight of water, wading with movements as exasperatingly slow as a deep-sea diver's.

Bee, he said, but made no sound. It was there, the heart of the thing, the centre of this milky fluid air that pulsed about him; it came to him in waves like pulsing blood. Bee? It was pouring out of the kitchen, light and sound, one silvery, the other dark, velvet dark, cold. The whole kitchen was filled with it, so that there was no shadow, not even under things or behind things—the light had flowed into every crack like slow water.

Bee was there, standing facing the door, her bare feet firm in the very centre of the maze, so that its silvery lines curled around her like petals round the stamen of a flower. She was naked, shining whitely in the silvery dark, standing erect, her head thrown back. She was glaring at him triumphantly, her lips parted from her teeth, no humour in her face, only that deadly, triumphant grin.

'I've done it,' she said. 'I killed him. Sacrificed on his own altar.'

Bewildered he stared at her. He saw that in

141

one hand she was holding a knife, a knife with a slender triangular blade, the blade did not shine in the light—it was dark, from point to hilt, with blood.

'I killed him,' she said again. 'I had to, you understand. I couldn't let him do what he was going to do—and I had to save the child. So I killed him on his own altar.'

He did not speak. His whole body was rigid with horror, and his mind struggled like a mad animal, trying to make sense of what could not be. Her slender body was distended from the bottom of her ribs to her pubis with the elongated, familiar shape of the child. She was six months gone in pregnancy. She shook her straight dark hair back from her shoulders and lifted the knife to show him and smiled. 'It's all right,' she said. His eyes followed the blade, fascinated, and he saw a single drop of blood fall from its point to the gathering pool on the floor.

Paul put his hands over his eyes and tried to scream, but he could make no sound, no sound at all, any more than he could have cried out under water. He felt something reaching out for him, pouring out towards him to overwhelm him and drag him down too, and he struggled with all his will, though he was as still as if bound hand and foot, unable to make any move. He remembered asking Clifford, is madness catching? and that detached part of his brain still reasoned, a long way off, that this

142

could not be happening, that it made no sense.

He felt cold, very cold, and as his bare skin bristled all the way down his front he forced himself to open his eyes again and face what had to be faced. Bee stood before him, staring at him with fear—the thin, haggard Bee he had fallen asleep with, her short curls disordered by her restlessness, her hands outstretched to him, empty and imploring.

'Paul, help me,' she whispered. He made a step forward reaching towards her, and she broke out of whatever restraint held her and ran to him, clutching at him with icy, trembling hands.

'It's all right, Bee,' he heard himself saying. 'It was only a nightmare. Everything's all right.'

'No,' she cried, 'No, look—Paul, look. Oh God, I can't bear it!'

He looked. The kitchen was as he had always known it, their ordinary, everyday kitchen; he had dreamed, hallucinated, imagined everything. But on the floor in the middle of the maze pattern was a pool, spreading towards the sink with the slight slope of the ground, of blood, dark and glinting in the starlight from the window.

'No, Bee, it isn't really there,' he said, clutching her as fiercely as she clutched him, his brain struggling with sanity. 'You're imagining it—there's nothing there.'

'You see it too!' she cried in terror.

'No! No! There's nothing there!'

'Paul look. Oh God.' Her voice descended into agonised despair. He followed her gaze downwards and saw against his will the wet footmarks she had made, and the dark stain of it on her white feet.

*　　　*　　　*

There was nothing to explain it. There was nothing they could say either to each other or to anyone outside, no comfort they could offer their stretched reason. Shuddering with cold and fear Paul had forced himself to mop up the dark mess from the floor before, with a sense of hopelessness they had gone back to bed to cling to each other and doze fitfully through what was left of the night. Waking in the morning had seemed to offer, for a time, a small hope. They woke unwillingly, hesitated to look at each other, and on looking and reading the memory and realisation in each other's faces they could not speak.

Perhaps it had been, if not a dream, then some kind of joint hallucination. Without speaking, Paul had prepared to investigate, had gone downstairs with growing hope and apprehension, walked slowly to the kitchen, and seen, his soul performing a sickening loop inside him, the smeary stain on the floor, the red-streaked wetness in the sink, the reeking cloth, imperfectly rinsed out. There was nothing to explain it, no way of making it make sense to his poor battered brain. He shook his head, and remembered how often in recent weeks he had seen Bee doing the same thing. He understood now.

Well, perhaps he could spare her some of the horror, even if he could not free himself of it. He washed the cloth out, shuddering, under the tap, wiped the floor until it was clean, and ran water into the sink for a long time until there was no trace left. He washed his hands, too, stopping only when he found himself wincing at the rasp of the scrubbing brush. Then slowly, slowly he made his way upstairs. He would tell her it had never been, that they had imagined it. Bad enough that they should both have imagined the same thing, and something so terrible: but better than that it should have been real.

He entered the bedroom and his eyes went straight to Bee's lifted to meet him. She must have read his intention before he spoke, for she shook her head, tears starting in her eyes, and put her fingers to her lips. Then, slowly, she drew back the bedclothes and, his eyes following the direction of hers, he began very quietly to weep.

'Oh Bee,' he said at last in pity. Her feet were scaled with dried, rust-coloured blood, black where it had caked between her toes and under her toenails.

CHAPTER TEN

It seemed like part of the same nightmare when Louise 'phoned only half an hour later to say that Clifford was unconscious after a heart attack.

'I'm at the hospital now—oh please come, Paul, please,' she said. She was crying, and it was hard to understand her.

'We'll come straightaway—where are you?' he managed to reply, and a moment later, much sobered and brought back to the real world, he was telling Bee. She only nodded, almost as if she had expected it.

'We'd better go,' she said. 'We may be too late to see him.'

He stared, and then hurried to get dressed.

He was in a private room, and Louise met them in the corridor outside it. Her face was blotched and swollen with crying; she was wearing no make-up, and her hair evidently not been done that morning. She held out her hands to Bee, and Bee took her in her arms and held her tightly for a moment. Then, released, Louise said,

'I couldn't wake him this morning. I thought he was play-acting at first, then I noticed how strange his breathing was. I telephoned for an ambulance and they brought him straight here.'

'How is he?' Paul asked. Louise couldn't answer for a moment, and then managed only to say,

'Bad.'

Bee didn't answer at all. Her face was grave, steady. They followed Louise into the room where, attended by a nurse, Clifford lay under an oxygen tent on the high bed, connected by wires to a cardiograph.

'They have all the best equipment here,' Louise whispered, as if to console herself. 'If anyone can do anything, they can.' Paul reached out for her hand and she pressed against him, shivering a little, like a rabbit. Bee walked over to the bedside and looked down at the still figure of her lover with calm eyes. His skin was white as wax, blue-white, with that firm, shiny look of wax that comes in death. The lines of authority and thought had been smoothed away—he looked younger than he had, as young as he had looked years ago when she had first fallen in love with him. Then, she remembered, he had slept with a small frown between his golden brows, as if sleep were a serious problem that needed thinking about.

There was no frown now. He slept as if he had given up all responsibility for his life and the problems that had beset it, relaxed as a child that has never known the weight of guilt and the human burden of fallibility. His fair hair, untidy and ruffled into a crest, was damp round his brow where his face had been washed for him: only in childhood and in death, that loving touch. We wash our dead as a cat washes its kittens.

'He hasn't regained consciousness, then?' Paul was asking Louise, still in a church whisper, as if, Bee thought, it could disturb him now!

'Not yet,' Louise whispered back. 'Does that mean he's very bad? He will get better, won't he?'

'Of course he will,' Paul whispered the automatic assurance. Louise, for what reason she did not know, turned to Bee for the final word.

'Bee, he will get well, won't he?' she pleaded. Bee lifted her eyes from contemplation of Clifford's face. She regarded Louise steadily, but she didn't speak; Louise read in her calm eyes the confirmation of what was already in her own mind—he will die. She began to cry again, loudly and harshly, and Paul put his arm round her and escorted her gently out.

Bee watched them go indifferently, and then sat down at the bedside to resume her contemplation. She had the best right to be here, she thought, for she had known him, as well as one human can know another. She mused gravely on the years they had spent together that would end so abruptly here. Already he was beyond her, unreachable, breathing an air that was not of this world, yet she felt that he was close under the surface, perhaps still aware of her, though unable any more to tell her so.

So, you broke faith at last. Mine to the end, but the end of you, not of me, leaving me masterless, undirected. I was a part of your fate; without you I have no identity. All down the years they had loved, first one, then the other, their orbits inter-related but never intersecting, like the earth's and the moon's for while he pursued his own fate, she pursued him. His body, still young and almost perfect—but for the malfunctioning heart, the coughing, choked-up engine—which had taken such delight in hers; his mind which she knew so well she could walk in and out of it like her own house; what more? If there had been more to him, it might not all have seemed so futile.

But he was still here, by however small a margin. In a little while he would be dead, and this body would no more be him than any other corpse. He would be gone, utterly, absolutely, for ever, as if he had never existed, and all that they had done together and meant to each other would be gone too. If only they could have had a child: a child was literally, actually, a part of you, some of the cells of your own body. No love without a child, no eternity, no future, no life. As he is dead already, so am I: a barren woman is death. She is pointless, futureless, dead as this man who will never think of speak again.

We die, you and I, here, in this room. What comes after will be merely clearing the stage of the scenery and props. Our lives will be as meaningless as if we had never lived. We might just as well, my dear, not have bothered. She had a feeling of impending doom. It was almost tangible, as a gathering dark at the wrong time of the day precedes a storm. Whatever was happening to her was coming towards its climax, and Clifford's pointless small death was a part of it, the beginning of the end.

She was suddenly aware of loneliness, filling her like hunger. It is lonely to die. She touched the perfect wax hand that lay outside the covers, and it rebuked her with its stillness. Die your own death, that is the one thing we must do alone. Together in the attitudes of love, embraced between the sheets, locked in all the battles of human will, there is always the knowledge of that last act that must be performed, and performed alone. I am alone in my death as you will be in yours. Clifford, you should have loved me more while we had time. All the hours we did not spend together, all the time we wasted being with people we did not care for and doing things we did not really need or want to do; and now there is no time left, in this world or any other, to be together.

The nurse stirred, examined the dials, felt the pulse of the other limp hand. Her eyes met Bee's, equally unconcerned. *Not yet*, her eyes said, *but soon.* I have said goodbye, Bee thought, though he'll never know it. Nothing more to do. She got up stiffly, feeling tired, and left him to die alone.

* * *

He did not die then. He lingered on, still unconscious, into the afternoon, keeping Louise on the spot, though without hope. It had the good effect, at any rate, of numbing her a little to the death. At one time he seemed to rally a little, and it looked as though he were drifting upwards to the surface and might break through into consciousness; but though he floated just under the surface for more than an hour, then he sank again, waterlogged this time, to the bottom, to the end. He died at last, without ever regaining consciousness, at tea-time, and Paul was able to take Louise home through the cold October dusk—by her own request, to her own home.

'I don't feel it yet,' she said later, crouching by the fire in her sitting-room. In her hands was a cup of coffee. On the hearth by her foot was a tumbler of brandy. Bee and Paul sat near, similarly provided, speaking sometimes, listening to their own breathing at others. Clifford made a fourth in presence: not that any of them believed in ghosts or even the survival of the soul—only that he had always been the fourth, and it was hard not to expect him to come in at any moment.

'I can't feel he's dead,' Louise said. 'It doesn't seem reasonable. It was so sudden—I feel cheated, somehow, as if I haven't been given proper warning. I feel I ought to sue somebody, like the time they cut our gas off because they said we hadn't paid a bill, and we had but they'd lost it. It isn't *fair*.'

'You probably won't feel it for some time. Be glad of that,' Paul said. 'Time enough when it does come.'

'He feels close,' Louise said. She sounded either surprised or complaining. Bee shivered convulsively and looked around at the familiar room, lit softly with lamps and firelight. Not his home, nor hers. This house was all Louise's and she was left with it, instead of the warm man she had called husband, who had never been hers. Bee found Louise grisly, like the evidence of a car-accident, the severed leg lying in the road. She ought to have been cleared away like the rest of the corpse. It was indecent that she should be left here with all the semblance of life, as if she might get up and walk off of her own accord.

'I never really knew him you know,' she said next. 'He wasn't a person you could get close to—I don't think anyone in all his life understood him. I don't suppose he wanted anyone to understand him. He was a closed-up person. He never said anything about how he felt or what he really thought about things. If

152

you asked him a question, you were as likely to get a joke in reply.'

They talked on through the evening, Louise's monologues and Paul's brief comments from time to time. Bee sat silent, shivering from time to time. This was a hiatus, like the quiet at the eye of the storm, trouble behind and trouble to come but here, now, quiet for a while. Louise talked about Clifford, the Clifford she knew and, after a while, the Clifford she had invented for herself, talking him out, moulding his memory to fit her ideas of him. She talked her way through him, talking him into the past so that, though she may mourn him, and feel lonely, and feel cheated, she would never after this evening miss him, for she would have distorted him, rewritten him, cancelled him out. You need never have lived, Bee thought to herself. If you had not existed, someone would have invented you as plausibly as yourself.

'I'm afraid that, after a while, your patience will wear thin,' Louise said later. 'I know that everyone's good to a bereaved person at first, but then they drop them, just when they may need friends most. It can take years to get over it.' She's full of these little facts and figures, Paul thought. She said the same sort of thing about Bee. Where does she get them from? Magazines, most likely.

'That won't happen to you, Louise,' he said aloud. 'Even if you count us out, seeing we're friends of yours as well as of Clifford's, you'll still always have people clamouring to meet you. Look at all the things you did, things you organised. You've hundreds of friends. You could never be alone.'

'I'm afraid,' Louise said. 'That's what I'm afraid of—of being alone, of getting old alone. I don't want to be one of those people who dies alone in a house and no-one knows for weeks until the milkman reports it to the police.'

Paul got to his feet and went over to her chair, squatted beside her and put his arm round her.

'Don't be silly, Lulu,' he said gently. 'You won't be alone. If no-one else, there'll always be me—Bee and me,' he added. 'We would never see you lonely.'

'Don't leave me, will you Paul,' she pleaded. 'Promise you'll never leave me.'

'I promise, I promise,' he murmured, stroking her hair. Bee watched them without rancour. She imagined just for a moment that Clifford was beside her, that they were both dead and watching a scene that would take place some months or years hence.

'I always knew they'd get together in the end,' Clifford said to her, and she said.

'They should have each other. They'll be happy now.' A waste, she thought, that they should have married their respective partners. If she had not married Paul and Clifford had not married Louise, they could have married each other and been happy, and none of this would have happened. But with great clarity she knew that Paul would not have chosen Louise instead of her. He had wanted her, and only as a result of having had her would he one day marry Lulu.

She got up and went to the window, leaving the tableau in the firelight, and drew back the curtain a little. The night was as brilliantly clear and distant as crystal, a great white moon swimming in a black sky, the air bitterly cold and ringing; there was frost, glittering along the railings and riming the black, dead leaves that were rotting in the gutters. She knew already what tomorrow would be like, clear and cold, with a wintry sun, perhaps a little soft fog later, smelling of woodsmoke or blackberries. She remembered the walk they had taken down to the river, felt Clifford's hand holding hers as they lagged behind the other two; always the only company they wanted was each other and a stick to slash at the grass as they walked. The first leaves had been falling then. There had still been some hope of escape.

But she felt comforted. It seemed to her then that time was not a stream that moved in one direction only, taking you ever further from perfection and pleasure, an irreversible mistake. She felt that all times are present, that whatever happens, happens for ever, somewhere, only needing to be reached for.

Somewhere she and Clifford were walking along the riverbank still, and would walk always. Time was a great roll of fabric that could be folded this way and that, gathered in or spread out, wrapped around you, close and comforting. *I am here for ever. It is not wasted.* There were ways back. It was not finished once and for all, for if only you could find the door, you could fold time back on itself and live again.

'Bee,' Paul called her softly. She turned and looked at him, where he sat still with an arm round Louise, who was crying softly. 'What are you thinking of?' he asked, not meaning it literally.

'It's of no consequence,' she said, smiling, and she meant it just as it was said.

CHAPTER ELEVEN

The day of the funeral was cold and grey, the sky overcast, blank and pale like blind eyes, with a cold, gusty wind threatening rain. The church was stuffily hot, but smelled cold, the dead odour of candles and incense and dust. The gusts of hot air that came up through the elaborate iron heating vents seemed to stifle without warming; the light that filtered through the Victorian stained-glass was lurid and inadequate. All that was alive in the church was in the flowers, massed everywhere: chrysanthemums, vivid acid-yellow, aching white, tawny gold like lions' manes, glowing red-gold, orichalcum, the precious metal beloved of the Atlanteans. They smelled of rain and earth and all that was living; and they themselves were dying.

The church was full, for he had many friends. Eyes were bent respectfully on the coffin on its covered bier; dark suits and coats, black ties and dull hats signified that these people had loved the man in one way or another. Bee looked about her, amazed again at the way people behaved. What a curious ting we do. He is dead, we perform a ritual. Is it because we fear what people will say of us? or does it offer some comfort? Not to me. Not to me. But to Louise? She was dressed all in black, black dress, black coat, black hat with a half-veil, and she was crying. To Bee it looked routine, a polite, elegant snuffling into a handkerchief, as was expected of her. She must have planned it, Bee thought, for why else would she have had a handkerchief to snuffle in? Like everyone else Bee knew, Louise habitually used paper tissues.

Because of what people might say, she went along with the service, standing and kneeling and sitting and murmuring responses. Only when they sang did it affect her—tears filled her eyes, her throat seized up, her heart lurched inside her. Paul felt for her hand to squeeze it and she drew it away from his sharply. It's the *music*, she wanted to tell him, that's all. The *music*.

They sat, and the vicar spoke, solemnly, sadly, respectfully, and with a subdued Christian hopefulness, just as he ought. He is dead, Bee thought. The four strong strands of our lives were woven together like a rope, and now he has snapped, we begin to unravel. We were all plaited together, we have always been. She remembered her schooldays, and Paul, mending a puncture in her bicycle outside the school gates, oblivious of the giggles and stares of the other schoolgirls coming out. She had always admired him for his imperviousness to other peoples' opinions, until she discovered it was because he was not sensitive enough to perceive them.

Then there were her dancing days, and Clifford, distant and desirable, giving her crumbs of praise and admiration as one might give a tip to a cloakroom attendant; taking her body casually out of an idle whim, more because she wanted him than because he wanted her. And her university days with Louise, the two of them curled up on the battered sofa in the Union Bar, discussing sex and literature and philosophy and clothes.

And all the days since, shrinking and contracting her life up to the full stop that was Clifford's death. He was dead, and there was an end to all his possibilities; and what of her, what was there for her? Spilt from his cupped hands, she would disperse like water, formless, soaked up by the great desert that was all of Time.

A final hymn. She stood bleakly through it, unhearing and unseeing. The bearers walked, heads down, to take up their burden again, and the congregation followed them out to their cars. Most of them dispersed then. The churchyard was long ago filled to capacity, and the cemetery was fifteen minutes' drive away. Most of the guests welcomed the opportunity not to go to the graveside, got into their cars and dawdled behind the hearse until they could decently get lost.

The graveside service was short, and during it the rain began, fine and drifting and cold, penetrating their clothes and hanging like silver fleece over the heaped flowers. Louise had never ceased to cry dutifully, but when the coffin was lowered and the familiar, deadly words trembled on the soft, damp air she began to weep in earnest. The few gathered at the graveside looked at her in uncomfortable pity, and then down at their own feet while she sobbed in the sudden clarity of realisation, her face ugly with crying, her hands twisting at her wet handkerchief while her eyes were fixed on the gaping hole in the earth.

At the sound of the earth pattering on the wood of the coffin, Bee looked away. Paul glanced at her. She had turned her face up to the sky so that the rain fell on it, running over her cheeks, and no-one but him would know she had not been crying. He hated this business. He waited only until the last words were said and the coffin covered over, and then put his arm round Louise and urged her away, leaving the men whose business it was to fill in the grave and make all decent, hiding the newly raw earth with flowers. He felt jumpy and irritable, and it soothed him somewhat to have Louise to care for. She allowed him to draw her away, though he could feel her reluctance, as if she was leaving Clifford there for the last time. Bee followed them, calmly, dry-eyed. Paul both approved and disapproved. She had already said goodbye; but it seemed unwomanly that she did not weep.

*   *   *

It was late before they got home, for Louise did not want to be left alone at first. Later, with a change of mood, she refused to have them stay the night with her, and demanded they go and, promising to 'phone the next morning, Paul had obeyed, catching Bee at the door. Her haste in leaving had seemed to him indecent. Once home, Bee went to the kitchen to put the kettle on, and Paul followed her, feeling his anger rising. He watched her for a time moving about the kitchen, and then said abruptly,

'I don't know what you've got to say to
160

excuse your behaviour.'

'My behaviour?' she said dully.

'To poor Louise. You were distinctly lacking in sympathy. You were almost out of the door before she had said goodbye.' He put his hand to his head and rubbed it. There was a pressure inside it, a pressure on his ears that made him feel slightly dizzy. It made a kind of buzzing noise in his ears. 'It's all of a piece with your selfishness, I now—'

'My selfishness?' Bee turned to look at him. She seemed far off, like an image seen through crystal. 'I don't understand you. We are all bereaved.'

'Louise was his wife,' Paul said angrily.

'She never knew him. She was his wife, and you were his friend, but I loved him, I knew him, and I loved him.' She came a step towards him. He put both hands to his ears as the buzzing increased. 'What's the matter?'

'I don't know—dizzy—ringing in my ears,' he muttered. She was standing in front of him now, very close, her white face framed for him by the blackness outside the window. The street lamps must have gone out for it to be so black out there. The wind was rising too—he could hear it moaning high up round the house, and rattling the window-panes. Wind but no rain. It ought to rain. Rain would be a blessing after—

After what? His thought didn't seem to lead anywhere. He felt confused, fuddled. If only

161

this pressure, buzzing would pass, he would be able to think straight. Or was he—was he beginning to be affected too? Whatever was making Bee strange, was it getting to him at last? He thrust the thought from him with all the strength of his will. No, he was dizzy, that was all. Cling to what made sense. Hungry, that was it! He was hungry, he hadn't eaten all day, that was why he was dizzy. A gust of wind shook the window angrily, and its constant voice outside rose to a hooning pitch. There was not much time left. Her white face framed in its black hair was before him still and he remembered his anger.

'You loved him? What do you mean, you loved him? What exactly does that mean, eh? I think I'm beginning to get the picture, I think I'm beginning to see quite a lot of things I should have seen before. How long has it been going on, this *love* of yours? and why didn't you see fit to tell me about it before? No, you don't need to answer that, I think, I know the answer. I do, don't I? You kept it secret because you were having an affair with him, weren't you? I've been a fool not to have seen it before! You've been carrying on behind my back all this time,—-and laughing at me too, you lousy bitch!'

His rage mounted, and he grabbed her by the arms and shook her. 'How long? Answer me! How long? How many years? And the baby— that was his, wasn't it? You were carrying his baby, you whore, you tried to pass it off onto me!'

'No!' she shouted. 'Paul, what are you talking about? What's happened to you? Paul!'

She wriggled against him, trying to free herself, while he glared at her, gripping her upper arm and shaking her furiously as the wind was shaking the house, while his anger surged inside him like a tide, filling every corner of his mind. He would kill her, the lousy bitch, kill her! He switched his hands from her arms to her throat, and as he did the ground lifted under him, a long ripple like an animal shrugging something off its back. Plates and cups fell to the ground, smashing to pieces, furniture slid and toppled, pots clanged and bounced on the stone floor, and with a noise like fabric ripping a long crack zipped snakelike up the wall, and across the ceiling, gaping open, showering them with fragments and plaster dust.

It all happened in a second, and in that second Paul forgot everything but fear. As the ceiling groaned open, he grabbed Bee and leaped for the back door, fought with it for a desperate half-second, and flung himself with her out into the safety of the garden, losing his balance and falling with her onto the grass. For a long moment he lay still, Bee half underneath him, his arm over his head and his face in the wet grass, the smell of the damp earth in his nostrils, waiting for the smashing pain in his

163

back as the house tumbled onto them. But there was nothing, nothing, no sound, silence.

After a moment he heard a dog bark distantly, and cautiously he lifted his head. Everything was as it should be, the quiet garden, wet from the afternoon's rain, lit by the artificial twilight of the street lamps. He looked round at the house. That was normal too, a slice of light falling from the open door like a wedge of cheese into the shadows of the walls. The rain had stopped, and there was no wind. The night was still, and cold.

He sat up. 'Bee?' he said cautiously. She sat up too, rubbing her ribs. 'Bee, are you all right?'

'Yes,' she said uncertainly. 'You fell on top of me. You hurt my ribs. Otherwise—'

'Not broken?' he asked anxiously.

'No. I'm all right.'

He looked away towards the house again. What had happened? An earthquake? But—? Or had he imagined it? The blood burned his cheeks at the thought. He glanced at Bee, but her face was neutral. How could he ask? Supposing he had imagined it? He couldn't give himself away. He stood up and walked unsteadily towards the house. It took all his courage to go in, to look in at the kitchen door, and as he did, his heart contracted inside him. Everything was normal, as it should be. Everything in its place, the kettle Bee had put on just beginning to boil, sending wisps of steam out of its ordinary domestic nose. No cracks, no broken crockery.

He jumped as Bee came up behind him and touched his shoulder. She looked past him at the kitchen, and then their eyes met cautiously, questioningly. Paul opened his mouth to speak, but she forestalled him.

'Don't say anything. For God's sake don't say anything.'

'Bee—'

'Please Paul! Don't say *anything*!'

She brushed past him and stepped down into the kitchen, walking round the maze, to the stove, where she lifted the kettle off the gas and filled the teapot. She set it to warm, found cups and saucers and set them on the table, poured a little milk into each, put the milk back in the 'fridge, took the tea-strainer from the draining-board, and poured two cups. Paul watched her from the doorway, dry-mouthed, unspeaking, his mind and body one as hollow as the other. Then carrying the two full cups Bee walked past him into the house and upstairs towards the bedroom. She was right, of course, that was the place to be, the safe place. A good night's sleep. It had been a long day, a long emotional day.

But still he could not move. The house was quiet, too quiet, as if it was holding its breath. Outside it was quiet too. The rain had not begun again. What had happened to him? He blinked, and his eyes burned with tiredness,

165

and he rubbed them wearily. The movement released him from his frozen stance, and almost naturally he turned away from the door, reaching his hand towards the light switch. As he switched off the light, he glanced back automatically into the kitchen and saw, in the fraction of a second between the light and the dark, something white fluttering down from the ceiling.

Petal? or plaster?

Or imagination? He rubbed his eyes again and, trying not to feel the open black hole at his back, walked along the passage and up the stairs. The bedroom seemed a haven, the curtains closed, the bedside lamps filling the room with a cosy, rosy glow. Bee was sitting on the edge of the bed sipping her tea, and he sat down beside her, putting one arm round her thin shoulders, and taking his cup in his other hand. The hot, fragrant drink stimulated and calmed him, tasting as it did of normality and home, the gently repetitive action of lifting and sipping soothed him and relaxed him. In between sips he stared into the cup, at the gentle movement of the liquid, at the tender snippet of steam that lifted from its glinting surface. At the end of the drink he would be ready for sleep. At the bottom of the cup lay peace.

They put their empty cups aside at the same time and, still without a word, began to undress. Paul tried not to look at Bee, in pity for her thinness, but as he was about to get into bed, he noticed the bruising on her arms. Had he done that? No, surely if he had left a mark it would only be a red mark as yet. Bruises took time to come out. Quietly he crossed the room to her and, taking her gently by the arms he turned her towards him. She looked up at him apprehensively.

No, these were old bruises. But, dear God, where did they come from? Almost from shoulder to elbow her thin white arms were disfigured with bruises of various hues and various stages of development, some freshly blue, others black, others yellowing round the edges as they passed off.

'Bee, where do they come from? What have you been doing to yourself?' he said in horror. 'I've seen you bruised before, but this is terrible! I had no idea—I thought you'd stopped.' The words of Peter Cudlipp came instantly to his mind, that the self-inflicted wounds would almost certainly increase in gravity. What was the next stage? These could hardly be worse—she must then pass on to something else. Tenderly, with one hand, he stroked her left arm. 'Poor Bee. How did it happen? Can you tell me?'

She looked up mutely into his face with a mixture of doubt and fear, and then slowly turned her head to look at her other arm, which he was still holding with his left hand. He lifted his fingers one by one, and then carefully,

167

gently placed them on her arm again; and then again, in a different place, he placed his hand, and removed it. He saw, but he did not believe. Again and again he tried. Why hadn't he noticed before? The bruises fell all in a similar pattern; and the pattern fitted his fingers exactly.

*   *   *

What is happening to me? Paul sat down on the edge of the bed, wearily, rubbing his face as if the action would reassure him that he existed, and in the shape he remembered. Remembered? It seemed his memory was no longer his own. He didn't make those marks, he couldn't have! To have marked her like that, he would have had to virtually drag her round the room while she struggled: the bruises were almost bone-deep. And yet, and yet—he had seen the walls crack, felt the earth heave, seen Bee, heard her—

He sat bolt upright as the memory came back to him. Black hair, she had black hair. It was not Bee he had seen, but a black-haired woman with Bee's voice, Bee's voice saying 'I loved him'. No, it must have been Bee, but loved whom? Clifford? Somehow he didn't think so. He remembered that other time, the time she spoke to the man she imagined, and what Peter Cudlipp had said of his conversation with her. That's right, that's

168

right. Hold onto that. It was Bee who was ill, not him. That was reality. That, and Louise, bereaved, grieving. That was something he could do. Hold firm to the things that could be done.

Bee came back and, avoiding his eyes, climbed into bed and lay down on her back, pulling the sheet up to her chin like the coy heroines of old films; but there was nothing coy about her. She was cold and rigid, in the grip of some pain that he now saw reached back for years, something that was growing like a cancer inside her, swallowing her up until it was all there was. Paul switched the light off and got into bed. In the new, ringing darkness he felt the house stirring and breathing around him, gathering itself for the long night.

CHAPTER TWELVE

Had the question been put to him hypothetically before the event, Paul would not have expected to miss Clifford as much as he did. He was not a person who thought very deeply about relationships, taking very much for granted what was the case, and only worrying about it—as with his relationship with Bee—when it changed.

But losing Clifford seemed to take some basic support from him. He felt now very much on his own, left like the last survivor of a fighting unit to take on the enemy single handed. He felt now that Clifford had been on his side, had shared the responsibility, especially for Bee. There was no-one now on whom he could count for help, to whom he could go for advice or merely to discuss what was happening. Louise was a friend, of course, but even had she not been taboo by reason of her bereavement, he would never have felt she was a person who could help. Rather she was a person who had to be helped, an additional liability at a time when he was struggling to keep his head above water.

He felt that had Clifford not died, he might at last gone to him to ask his opinion over—he could only call it their joint hallucinations. Strain, Cliff would have said—you're under a lot of strain and you've started imagining things too. That had to be the case. The alternative was—well, there wasn't an alternative. Bee had been sick for a long time, and now he was catching it too.

After all it had never happened in broad daylight, only things that could be explained away. He discounted the blood—they had only just woken up after a night of bad dreams. Of course, there was the possibility that it was not Bee who was sick at all, but him—that he had imagined everything himself without her aid, even imagined her seeing the same things as he had seen. That was both more and less

170

worrying than that she was ill. He wondered if it would help to call up that man Clifford had put them on to—Peter Cudlipp. Perhaps even just telephone him and ask his advice. But what could he ask him? He had said (hadn't he?) that Bee should be admitted for treatment. Asked again, he would probably only repeat his former opinion.

And what if there turned out not to be a Peter Cudlipp, what if he, Paul, had imagined all that as well? It was a terrifying prospect. Once doubt was cast on what you knew to be reality, there was no stopping it. It was like pulling a loose thread—before you knew where you were, the whole fabric had frayed, running in all directions and leaving you with nothing to grasp, nothing at all. He *had* to take certain things as having been real: but where did he draw the line? Sanity turned out, after all, to be no more than a matter of confidence.

Paul and Bee lay side by side in the bed, not touching, staring at the ceiling, both unable to sleep. The room was lit by the first slanting rays of the bright moon outside, and the light made Paul nervous. Night was something to be feared, now, and lived through, for between lying down and getting up he would be unable to be sure what was real and what was not. Even the quality and quantity of light in the room—did he imagine the fluctuations? Would he again imagine that silvery, pulsing mist that left no shadows? He gripped the sheets hard

171

with his hands and lay by his sides and tried to be sure of what he knew.

Bee, beside him, was breathing lightly, as if she feared to disturb something. They had not made love since Clifford died: since that time, even that fierce splurge of energy seemed to have deserted her, and she was as light and brittle now as a dried leaf, empty of everything except patience. She seemed to be waiting. They spoke little to each other, never touched, tolerating each other as perhaps two animals in the same trap might.

He dozed, waking with a start to wonder if anything had started happening while he slept. The house was so quiet that the silence sang in his ears like the deafening roar of a waterfall. He felt dizzy, though lying down. He felt Bee stir and then sit up, and saw her bony profile suddenly cut out against the light. She sighed lightly and got up to go to the window where she drew aside the curtain to look out. He saw her crane her head to look up at the sky, as if she were trying to gauge the weather; then she came back and stood at the foot of the bed looking at him.

'I killed him, you know,' her voice came at last. Her face was in shadow and he couldn't see her lips move, but it was her normal voice, almost conversational.

'Yes,' he said.

'I killed him.' She thought for a moment. 'You saw me.'

'I know.' A pause. 'Who was he?'

'He was my lover. Oh, long ago, before I married, when I was a temple dancer. He was a priest, and a minister, and he loved power. He hated you, he hated all your party. He thought you effete, unfit to rule, so he worked at it: at your downfall.'

The nonsense flowed easily over his head. He heard it without effort and, more frighteningly, without surprise. As each broken phrase came to him he had a sense of already knowing it. Madness, madness.

'He wanted me as a priestess, he thought I'd bring him power. One night when we were making love he tied my hands and marked me for the god with the point of his knife. I screamed and fought, but he did it all the same.' Her voice grew lower and faded away at that point, as if she were remembering the small but sharp pain, and the humiliation of being forced. She turned her head a little and he could see the frown between her brows as she thought. Her eyes were closed.

'It was barbaric, all the temple customs were. He was not a cruel man, only ambitious. The next day I waited for him at the temple, and I cut my hands so that he could see how bloody and barbaric it was.'

'What did he say?'

'He laughed. He said I was better at it than he was, but then he came nearer and saw the bloody marks, and he was sorry. He cried, and

173

his tears fell on the wounds and washed away the blood. So he said I was his, because he had mingled his tears with my blood.'

A small smile touched the corner of her lips, a wry smile, and there were tears on her cheeks, seeping out from under the closed eyelids.

'You loved him?' he whispered, and it was hardly a question. He felt hollow, as if all his substance had been drawn from him, as if he had bled white. She had loved him. But this was madness, it was nothing.

'I belonged to him. Even after I married, I belonged to him. And I killed him. That's why it had to be me, because I belonged, I was his.'

'Why did you kill him?'

'I had to kill him, there was no other way. I knew what he planned to do. I couldn't allow him to destroy us all. Besides, there was the child—the child had to live. So I killed him. I think he knew—perhaps if I had not killed him then he would have killed me. But I think he knew.'

There was silence for a moment, and in the silence he could hear her breath, dragging now as if she were climbing a steep incline. She was near the end.

'He looked up as I came into his room. The moonlight fell across the bed like a blade. I came from the darkness, and he couldn't see me until I was close to him. He pushed himself up on his elbows, screwing up his eyes against the light, and he said who is it?

174

'I came close to him, and he smiled at me, he said, oh it's you, and then he saw the knife.' She tilted her face backwards, her throat straining with her desperate breaths. 'He looked at the blade, and then at me, and he gave a wry smile, as if to say, so that's it, is it? And then I struck.'

She sobbed, tears falling freely now, her voice faltering and clotting with the tears as she went on. 'He didn't struggle. He made no sound as I stabbed him, though his body arched and his hands went to the place as though he might press the edges of the wound together and make it not to be. But he groaned when I pulled the knife out, and it was terrible, it was like dying, that terrible cry—he felt betrayed.

'I stared at him as he clutched at his heart and writhed under the sheet, his eyes never leaving my face, though his face was contorted with pain. Then he lifted his hands all bloody and showed them to me, palms outmost, and he said—'

She paused for a long time, her face working as she tried to control her voice, relieving the old grief, the worst of all human pain. Then at last she went on: 'He could only whisper, he had no more voice than a whisper, and he cried, "strike again!" I cried out then, and jumped back from his bloody, reaching hands, clawing at me, trying to pull me back; his beseeching eyes and his tongue writhing in his mouth as he tried to speak. I didn't

175

understand, I turned to run, aghast at what I had done. And he whispered again, imploringly, "You did not strike cleanly. For pity, strike again".

'I understood then, but I could not do it. I was weeping, and my hands were limp. He was reaching for me in agony, and I placed my hands in his, my hands still holding the knife. He lifted them, and the blade to his throat, but he had no strength to do it, and I knew I had to, I could not let him suffer so. So I gripped the knife, and I cut his throat.'

He saw her sway with the force of her emotion, her wet and anguished face turned towards the moon; she had nearly done. 'The blood gushed out, and he fell limp on the bed, but his eyes were still open, and as I bent towards him I saw his lips move. He tried to smile; and he made no sound, but he said "My love!"

She sat down on the end of the bed and put her hands over her face. There was nothing either of them could say.

* * *

In the cold light of morning Paul considered everything as logically as he could, and his mind rejected logic and offered no answers. There was nothing he could do. Whatever this madness was, he was a part of it. He felt that he must know the ending.

176

The day was blazing hot, too hot for October; as were the days that followed. As if it were mirroring the break-up of his own personal world, the weather was going crazy. There were earthquakes all along the earthquake belt, one being as near as Northern Italy, and a tidal wave killed fifteen people in the West Indies. It was unseasonably hot and dry everywhere, except in California where a typhoon off the coast blew the damp sea-air inland and they had the wettest October on record. Elsewhere in America there were whirlwinds and droughts and great cracks appeared in the earth in Georgia. In Australia more than half of Canberra was blown flat by a hurricane, leaving thousands homeless.

In England people were eating strawberries and visiting the seaside and saying that the funny weather was probably caused by atom bombs and/or satellites.

In the unexpected heat, Bee sat out in the garden a lot. She had a book by her side, but it was never opened: she merely sat with her hands in her lap looking at nothing. She was like a person in the last stage of an illness, never moving or speaking. Her eyes followed Paul when he moved around her, but he did not touch her or speak to her. The tension was so great that it was as if a great press were being screwed slowly down on them, ever tighter and tighter, and they were frightened that any contact might shatter them entirely.

Paul felt himself gradually drawn in to the madness, to play a part that had been written for him. He did not need to ask what part it was. He knew, by the weight that daily fell more heavily on him, by his increasing sense of guilt what he had done. Bee's eyes followed him with mingled apprehension and hatred. *He had killed the baby*.

What was done was happening again, they were reliving the drama that had no place outside her mind, yet impinged more and more on reality until he could not distinguish between what he remembered and what he imagined. He had kicked the baby to death: that was his part in the drama. Anger and shame bowed his shoulders as he moved listlessly about the house. *Let it end*, he prayed in his mind. The waiting was intolerable. Let it end!

The strange things began to impinge also on daylight, and the sense of horror that held him dry-mouthed through each night became his daily companion also. In the hot strange days the walls cracked and opened like the mouths of wounds. The earth of the garden sank and shrank away from the house, exposing the foundations, and the walls began to lean dangerously, overhanging as if they would fall on the person passing beneath. The water in the lily pond disappeared one day under his very eyes, drawing down to the bottom of the pond and vanishing as if a plug had been pulled out, and on the dry, cracked bottom the leaves of the water-plants turned instantly brown. There was no water in the taps downstairs, and sometimes not in the upstairs taps either. They used it sparingly in case it should dry up altogether.

At night there were electrical storms, the sky lit almost to the brilliance of day by running, flickering blue lightening. There was rarely thunder, and never rain. They would lie in bed watching the violet shimmering sky and feeling the brimming silence over the world. Paul thirsted for rain, for cooling, life-restoring rain, for water, for winter. The heat made his head buzz. He got up and walked through the blue-streaked darkness to the bathroom and turned on the tap, with hope but without expectation. It worked. He filled the basin with water and rinsed his face, and then washed his hands, relishing the feeling of the cold water on his skin.

A movement behind him made him turn round. Bee stood in the doorway, staring at him with that same expression of fear and anger.

'The blood is on your head,' she whispered.

'No,' he protested, but her hand shot out, and she pointed, finger quivering, at the basin.

'You cannot *wash* your hands clean,' she said. He stared. The liquid in the basin was black in the imperfect light, and as he snatched his hands back from it he could see the dark

179

stains on his skin.

'No!' he shouted in horror. The basin of blood was lit briefly by the lightning. 'No!'

Bee was gone. Something happened. He heard almost without noticing the familiar burring hum filling the house. He did not want this. He remembered the other time. 'No!' he shouted again. They could not do this to him, he did not belong to them, believe in them, they were not his gods. 'No!'

But the fury gripped him. His body went rigid, and he felt the cold flow into it like black, infected blood, flow into every part of him. It bit at his mind, the frost falling inside his head and eating into each strand of thought. The house was like a living thing around him, pulsing with this alien force, drawing him down into its power.

He knew where she had gone. He followed her, his feet moving effortlessly, down the stairs and through the bowels of the dark house. She was there, a white figure, naked, curled face-downwards on the floor, crouched in the centre of the maze in a pool of her own blood. The blood frightened him, shocked him out of his dream-like state, for he had not expected it. He struggled with his cobwebby mind, forced himself to move, to run to her and lift her in his arms, lift her and cradle her head.

'Bee,' he said, 'Bee.' It was Bee after all. The dark hair he had seen spilled over her white back had been imagination, as had the blood.

180

There was no blood on the floor. Bee's thin body was in his arms, and it was the first time he had touched her for weeks. The touch reassured him: this was real. 'My darling,' he said. Touch is so comforting. Absurdly, for it cannot save you—yet two people facing death before a firing squad will put their arms round each other, as if they might ward off the bullets with their own fragile flesh.

He stroked her head, hopelessly. It's the end, he thought.

'Why,' Bee asked him. 'Why did you kill the child?'

'It was not my child,' he said. He knew now what had happened. He knew the whole story. Bee shook her head.

'It was not his child. You thought that, but it was not his child.'

'Then whose was it?' Paul asked, and the cold settled on him again as he waited for her to speak, because he already knew the answer.

'It was not any man's child,' she said. 'It was the child of the god, the One that was foretold. He would have saved the world.'

He made a harsh sound, that might have been a sob. Bee stroked his hand vaguely, as if to comfort him, but her eyes were far away.

'There's nothing more to be done,' she said. 'It is finished.'

CHAPTER THIRTEEN

Louise was worried about Bee and Paul. She had not seen them or heard from them for some time, and when she telephoned Paul's office to speak to him, and arrange to meet him at lunch time, they told her that he had not been in for several days, and that he had called to say his wife was ill and he was taking time off.

A very good excuse to 'phone them, Louise thought, but when she telephoned there was no answer. Her first thought was that Bee had been taken to hospital after all, and that Paul had gone to her, but when she got no reply to her subsequent 'phone calls, at various different times of the day, she began to feel there was something wrong.

It did not seem likely that Paul would fail to tell her if they had gone away. Suppose, though, Bee had died, and he was prostrate with grief? Or suppose Bee had had a fit of madness and stabbed Paul? She felt that it was time she investigated, that she should call round there and see what had happened. She couldn't understand why Paul had not contacted her. Something serious must be wrong.

She drove round to the house in the afternoon and stopped on the other side of the

182

road to observe the house from the car. It looked very quiet. Of course, even when there are people in a house, there is generally no visible sign from the outside, and yet the house gave the impression of being empty, as houses can do. She watched for a moment longer, and then went up the front drive and rang the door bell.

It clamoured in an empty way inside the house, and there was silence, no voice or footsteps or any sound. It was more than ever as if there were no-one there. She rang again, and then walked round to the side of the house, looking up at the windows and listening carefully. She tried the side door, but it was locked. She could not get into the back garden, because the gate was locked, and it was too high for her to see over, but there was no sound from there either.

It was very odd. She wondered if she had better contact the police—though she knew what they would say. They would say there was no evidence of anything being wrong, and they would come around and ring the bell and go away. People can go off without telling other people, and that isn't a crime. Puzzled, Louise turned away and walked back towards the car. As she passed out through the front gate she had the impression of eyes on her back and turned sharply, but saw nothing though she got the impression of someone moving hastily away from the window.

She hesitated, wondering whether to go back and ring again, and then decided not to. If they hadn't answered the first or second times, they were not likely to answer now. And in any case, she had probably only imagined it. The silence of the house was beginning to get on her nerves. But if there was somebody there, why were they avoiding her? It was very strange.

She had reached the car when she heard someone call her from across the road, and turning quickly she saw, to her disappointment, not Paul but the woman from the house next door, standing at her garden gate and beckoning her. Louise went back across the road.

'You a friend of theirs?' she asked in the tone of one who is going to demand compensation for the damage done by your dog.

'Yes,' Louise said stiffly. 'Do you know where they've gone?'

'Gone? They haven't gone anywhere that I know of.'

'Well there's no-one in now, anyway,' Louise said.

'No-one's gone in or out of that house for days,' the woman said, 'and I should know, because I've been watching for them. I wanted to have a sharp word with them, that's what.'

'I rang just now and nobody answered,' Louise said stubbornly. She didn't like the glint in this woman's eye.

'No, no doubt they wouldn't. Thought it was

the police, I expect. And I tell you, I'm thinking of calling the police right now. Talk about noise! Bangings and screamings and all sorts. Wouldn't surprise me if he hadn't murdered her.'

'Oh don't be so ridiculous,' Louise snapped. 'you've no right to say things like that.'

'You a friend of theirs?' she reverted to her earlier question, looking Louise up and down as if she were no better than she should be. 'Funny they wouldn't answer the door to you then, isn't it?'

'They're obviously out,' she said firmly.

'Oh no,' the woman shook her head with confidence. 'They're in there all right. I made sure of that. And I'm going to call the police if I don't see them by tomorrow. Because it's my opinion that there's some funny business going on in there. Black magic or something like that. You wouldn't believe the hullabaloo there's been some nights.'

'Look,' Louise dropped her aloofness and pleaded, 'when did you last see them?'

'I saw them both in the garden Wednesday, and I see *him* in the garden on his own Thursday, and that's the last.'

'Well they've obviously gone away,' Louise said firmly, keeping her thoughts to herself. 'They could easily have left during the night while you were asleep. Or any time when you weren't looking. You can't possibly have been watching the door twenty-four hours a day.'

185

The woman's smile was knowing and unshakeable. 'And you'd better watch what you say about them to other people, because you might find yourself in court for slander.'

The woman snorted derisively and walked away up her own path and into her house, slamming the door behind her. The Hagues' house was a detached house at the end of a row of semis, and there was a narrow strip of garden between them and this woman's side wall. It was highly unlikely she could have heard anything very much unless she'd been prowling round their garden.

But had there been someone at the window? Louise shook her head over the problem as she drove away. She decided to 'phone again as soon as she got home, and keep on 'phoning at intervals until she got an answer, or they contacted her some other way. And if she didn't hear anything in a few days, maybe she would call the police after all, and risk making a fool of herself. After all, that's what friends were for, wasn't it?

*   *   *

Paul watched Louise get into her car and drive away, and then he let the corner of the curtain drop and staggered back to the bed, collapsing onto it flat on his back. Bee, lying on the other side of the bed in a similar attitude, didn't move, but she groaned slightly.

186

Paul was sorry for Louise. He guessed it had been her ringing at intervals. He thought she would now 'phone again, but he could not see her. Not as he was. The room was unbearably stuffy, and it smelled pretty terrible too, of sweat and dirt. They were both grimy and sweaty, for there was very little water and they couldn't spare any of it to wash. Paul had not shaved for some time and his stubble irritated him like a hair-shirt. They had not eaten much either, but they didn't feel the need for it. It was too hot, and they spent most of the time lying on the bed, so they didn't get hungry. Bee's emaciated body was grey now, and her hair so tangled he doubted if she could have got a comb through it.

But it could not be long now. The day was oppressive, thundery, damp. The rain must come soon, and once the rain came there would be relief. It would wash away the dust, and the air would be cool again, and the earth green. The impending storm hung like anger over them; the world was still under it, waiting, cowering. Nothing moved, no animal, no bird, not even an insect stirred on the surface of the dry, shrunken earth. The sea had drawn back as if sucked into underground caverns, and on its bed were exposed the bones of long-drowned ships, and scattered wreckage under dry brown weed. The trees hung limp and still, their leaves flaccid, no breath or air stirring them. There was silence.

187

And the humans too were still, unable to move around in the heat. They lay spreadeagled, waiting for the coolness and watching the sky darken as the storm gathered. It would not be long. It was October the thirty-first.

*   *   *

By mid-day it was almost as dark as night, and the purplish-dark clouds covered the sky without a break from horizon to horizon. There was something frightening in the unseasonal darkness, something that stirred primitive fear in man. It was still stiflingly hot, and the air was so electric and so heavy that it made their hackles rise. The sea had gone almost out of sight, nothing but the stinking sea-bed and its litter visible for several miles out. Long-hidden treasures were being uncovered by the water's retreat, but there was no-one who could take advantage of it: all were prostrate with the heat.

The first breath of wind came suddenly and fiercely, but it brought no relief to anyone, for it was as hot as the breath of a furnace when the kiln door is opened; it came again, lifting the leaves on the trees briefly and rattling the fallen ones that had rotted in the gutter for weeks. The barometer was falling fast, and the violent changes in the air-pressure was making them feel giddy and sick.

Then it grew cold; the temperature dropped twenty degrees in ten minutes, changing the season from the summer they should not have had to the winter it should have been. The cold combined with the blackness was frightening: it was the face of death, it was what all creatures feared, this winter night that meant the end of all things. The wind began to rise, first rushing and rattling outside, its voice gradually rising to a moan as it streamed through the empty streets, lifting small pieces of debris high in the air and banging loose shutters fiercely against the walls.

They listened to it as they might listen to a prophet; there was no other sound but the rising voice of the wind; there was nothing they could do but submit to its increasing violence as it began to snatch at the fabric of the city, tear away anything loose, the unrepaired matter of the poor husband, flip heavy stone tiles from the rooves and fling them a hundred yards away against a wall, uproot small shrubs and sickly trees. It rose from a whine to a roar, buffeting the houses themselves and shrieking like demons round their frail safeness.

For hours there was nothing but wind and darkness, the sound of the wind and of its destruction. Now, in the dark, they clung together, all past discord forgotten in the face of the violent discord outside. Their house was as fragile as a bird's nest, and was all that stood between them and the violence, but they put

189

their arms round each other as if so they could hold off the black shrieking menace that was coming upon them.

If only it would rain! It seemed to them that the rain would be something benign, might temper the wind as a mother's voice might penetrate the evil mist clouding the thoughts of a maniac: but there was no rain, only the howling blackness.

Then the earth tremors began, mildly and far-spaced at first, but increasing in strength at closer intervals like the contractions of a woman in labour. The earth was being squeezed by more and more violent shudders as the night laboured to bring to birth—what? A new world, one in which there was no place for them, for their people, their culture, their pride, their civilisation, their cruelty and cleverness? But there had been beauty too, and love—were they to perish as well, everything to go down into the darkness that would never lift?

The rule was known to them both—when the earth shakes, get out of the house, get outside. But they didn't move. It seemed the worse alternative. Here in the house was a pocket of stillness within chaos, and, though it was doomed to fall, though they knew it could not last, they were unwilling to leave it while it offered them shelter.

Besides, they both knew now that there was no escape. It was the end, and nothing they

190

could do would save their lives nor the life of any of their people, not the least innocent child. They had seen the sea drawn back like the snarling lip of a dog, and they knew what it meant. It had happened before, in a small way, the shrinking sea hurling herself back at the land like an animal that had drawn back to spring. But this time the sea had almost disappeared, shrinking back miles and miles from the shore as if it were being drained by the mouth of a giant. When it returned, it would overwhelm everything, thousands of gallons of water hurtling down on them in a tidal wave miles high, travelling at the speed of a hurricane. It would destroy the whole land. There was no escape.

They lay still, listening to the sounds of destruction outside, the noise of the wind so high that they could not hear any sound of human voices, no crying or pleading or screaming or cursing. It was as if they were alone in the world, the only representatives of the race, who alone must bear the final burden. They pondered on the events of the past. Fear was almost outweighed by grief that this should be the end of their kind, the proudest, most brilliant of all animals that had trodden the earth, the inventive, the beautiful, the kind, the treacherous but utterly miraculous human kind. Had they been so evil that the world could no longer bear their footsteps? Surely there had been good to outweigh the bad?

Were all to perish, or would some, one or two survive in some far corner of the blue world to start again? Pray to the gods that it would be so, and pray also that they would remember the beautiful and useful things they had been taught, and forget the wickedness, the evil and destructive things. The earth shook again, angrily as a dog shakes a rat, and their walls split, and the plaster fell, the pictures painted on them crumbled and falling. The bright jewel colours spattered the floor like fallen flowers: the picture of the girl holding a bird on her palm, and the young man with the horse, and slant-eyed dancers—delicate, foolish pictures; the cleverness of this animal which would not save it now, now that the fury of the world was unleashed.

Time seemed no longer to exist for them. Perhaps they dozed while the world tore itself to pieces in its death agony. At one time the patch of sky outside the window was brilliantly lit as a rain of sparks and red-hot ashes poured down, fountaining out of the muzzle of the volcano almost a hundred miles away. Then the window panes were washed into blackness by an inky veil of black ashes, and the earth shook and grumbled while the wind howled them away.

And then she freed herself of his arms and sat up, her face only a lighter blur in the darkness that prevailed.

'What is it?' he asked. 'Don't let me go—I

don't want to die without you. Lie down again, there is nothing to be done.'

'No, wait, there is something. There is one thing left that can be done.'

'Nothing can save us,' he said.

'No,' she said, 'nothing can save us. But there is still something that can be done—one sacrifice left that the gods will accept.'

'Sacrifice,' he said bitterly. 'There is no sacrifice that will lay the sea back in its bed and still the wind. It is the end, I tell you.'

'It is the end, and we are going to die. But must the whole world die with us? Surely there may be someone saved, a few, a handful somewhere in the world to remember us and keep humankind alive? We can sacrifice for that.'

'What can we sacrifice?' he asked, but he already knew, and he shuddered and held out his hands to her. She spoke slowly:

'The child, the anointed one was killed, and for that sacrilege the world must die. It is not fit to live, the world that killed the god's child, it *must* be destroyed. I was the chosen vessel, and I failed; but I *was* the chosen one. I am holy, my life is sacred—it is a fitting sacrifice.'

'No!' he cried. He clung to her. He wanted her there beside him at the end.

'The god will accept my blood and mitigate the sentence. My people must die, but not the whole of humankind. I must do it, quickly, before the end.'

She got up from the bed and ran across the sloping floor of the room.

'Where are you going?' he whispered in agony.

'To the temple,' she said. 'It is fitting.'

'You'll never get there; don't go, please don't go!'

She made no sign of hearing him. She said, 'I hid the knife in the flowering creeper round the door of the temple. It will still be there. But I must do it now.'

She was gone. The wind, which had dropped, rose again with renewed force, howling as though tormented beyond endurance, ripping away the roof of the house so that for a moment he looked up into it, looking for the stars that were hidden. He knew what it was—it was the wind that ran before the water, forced forward by the great tidal wall that was galloping towards the city. He thought of her, struggling through the dark street to reach the temple, and suddenly he could lie still no longer. He got up and staggered to the door, calling her hopelessly, his voice drowned in the tumult.

Paul staggered to the door of the bedroom, his brain threshing like a machine out of gear, trying to make sense of what he was perceiving. The house was humming like a dynamo; shaking, too, like an engine racketing itself to pieces, and he himself was trembling in every limb. He knew where he must go—to the

194

heart of the disturbance, the focus through which the past was streaming in to be relived, passing through their fragile bodies like light through glass. He knew that there was something to be done there, something that was calling him down there.

The familiar and unfamiliar impinged at random on his senses making him feel sick and dizzy. The stairs and the hallway, the watercolour print on the wall at the foot of the stairs, the texture of the carpet, the old, frayed carpet they had brought from the other house to keep down the dust until they could afford a new one: and on the other hand, the battering tumult of the shrieking hurricane that was tearing the house to pieces, the throbbing of the power that was being released.

He reached the doorway of the kitchen and stopped there, leaning against the doorjamb weakly, his hand holding the familiar roughness of the damaged frame. The temple was bare and empty, part of the roof missing, the slab of the altar stripped: the cups and tripods and bowls had all been put away: as if any place could be safe now! From behind him the last few flowerets from the flowering creeper round the door were blown in between his feet to scatter on the dim marble floor. Through the kitchen window, he could see the peaceful twilight, the berberis hedge and beyond it the yellow candle of the street-lamp already lit in the road on the other side.

And she was there, her back to him, facing the altar, her hands held up above her head and between them the slender, triangular-bladed knife. And he knew then what it was he had to do. His hand went forward of its own accord to stay her, to avert the blow, but his tongue clove to the roof of his mouth. The blood was on his head, the blood of all their people, the guilt that could never be removed. But as she had one last act to perform, so had he. To consent, was his—and her blood would assuage the thirst in his soul. His heart flowed outwards in perfect love and submission, and the gleaming knife came down.

At once there was a terrible shriek that seemed to tear the fabric of the world. He flung his hands over his ears and staggered forward under it as under a blow; outside the maddened wind rose one last pitch, and as he fell forward on his knees he turned his face upwards and saw through the gaping roof one last glimpse of the stars as the clouds were torn away by the wind before the water.

*   *   *

Trembling, Paul rose again to his knees. There was stillness, such a stillness everywhere that he felt they must be alone in the world. The wind, the waves, the violence, all were stilled. The house was quiet. He felt light and shaky as if he had just recovered from a violent fever, but he felt also at peace. A great happiness filled him, a sense that he had been forgiven and washed clean. She had interceded. The blood had been accepted. It was all right.

The dark-haired woman lay there in the centre of the maze, peacefully on her back, her hair spread beneath her like a pool of water. Her face was quiet. He would not have called her back. Below her white face was a second mouth, a wide red mouth that ran from ear to ear, curving down her throat, and the dark pool under her head was not only her hair, but her blood.

He did not move or speak. He was transfixed with the glory of her face, the triumph and peace and love of the mother. And, as he looked, the figure changed subtly, blurred and shivered, became insubstantial, was fading away, for it did not belong to this world. And for the length of time that the image of light remains on the retina when the eye is closed, he saw Bee lying there, whole and unharmed and lovely, her eyes closed in sleep, before she disappeared, and there was nothing but a few petals, already turning brown, scattered about the floor.

CHAPTER FOURTEEN

Wharton and Darcy were the two men assigned to go round to the house to see what, if anything, was going on.

'Query suspected murder?' Wharton observed to the younger man. 'You can't get much cagier than that. Which is number 16?'

'It's the big one on the end, the detached house, corner of Bury Road.'

'Oh,' said Wharton, and then, with significance, 'Oh! Isn't that where that double-killing happened in '63 or '64?'

'I don't know. I wasn't even in the force then,' Darcy said.

'Never mind, lad,' Wharton said sternly. 'I wasn't around in 32 AD but I know the name of the lad that was crucified.'

Darcy made no comment, as indeed he was not meant to. Wharton's speech was like a woman's make-up—meant chiefly to cheer up himself. He continued to ponder.

'Yes,' he said at last, 'it was number 16. Rare bit of excitement, that was, at the time. Very grisly murder, husband slits throats of wife and lover; blood everywhere. Funny how a place attracts them, sometimes even when they don't know about it. They seem to have an instinct for where murders have been committed in the past.'

'Perhaps it's the ghosts hanging round,' Darcy said indifferently. He thought this particular case was going to be a non-starter. Unlike Wharton he had seen the neighbour who put in the complaint, and for his money she was a nosy, officious, interfering old bag. Probably she'd heard the couple having a bit of a barny, and took the rest out of the first novel she read.

In fact, if it hadn't been for coincidence of the couple's friend, the Mrs. Harwicke, reporting she hadn't heard from them for some time, it would probably have been ignored. As it happened, the neighbour had come in for the second time just before the woman had 'phoned, and the desk sergeant had put the two reports together and wondered.

The second time the neighbour had come to report that she'd seen the husband but not the wife, and that the husband had been out and bought several bags of cement—nothing else, despite the fact that the neighbour opined there couldn't be a scrap of food in the house.

They walked from the car, which they had parked round the corner in Bury Street, right round the two road boundaries of the house, just to get the feel of it. It was a big house, old and handsome, standing in its oddly-shaped patch of land on the corner of the two roads.

'Regency,' Wharton said appreciatively.

'Queen Anne,' Darcy corrected him without thinking, and went on, 'Been well kept up, too.

Somebody loves it.'

'If you like that sort of thing,' Wharton said, a little sour at having been corrected. 'Myself—' he let it hang.

'All quiet,' Darcy said. 'No sign of anyone. What's the procedure then?'

'Well we haven't got much help here,' he said, patting his pocket and making a grimace. 'Funny noises in the night, shufflings and shoutings and a scream. Wife disappears, according to neighbour. Refuse to answer the phone, according to friend. Husband last seen buying quantities of cement and scuttling back home with it. No, not much to go on.'

Darcy decided he was being ironical. 'Well?'

'Daft bugger, buying the cement like that.'

'Well, doesn't that point to the whole thing being blown up from nothing? Surely a murderer wouldn't be stupid enough to—'

'Course he would,' Wharton said derisively. 'This sort of job, they don't plan it. It comes upon them all of a sudden, the quick bash with the blunt instrument, and bingo, one body to dispose of. You don't *expect* them to show any aptitude for the crime.'

'So you think he's done his wife in and walled her up in the conservatory?' Darcy asked impatiently.

'Wait a bit, lad, I don't think anything yet. I'm simply here to find out. Let's see if this lad'll answer the door first. And if not, then we'll have to start thinking.'

200

They walked up the path and rang long and loud at the door bell. There was silence, a silence over the whole house. It seemed that it would not be answered. Wharton stepped back from the porch and tilted his head back to squint at the upper windows. He seemed quite relaxed and unconcerned.

'Can't imagine a double murder going on here, can you?' he said to Darcy conversationally. 'Too suburban and dull. Still, that sort of murder is hardly really a murder at all. *Crime passionelle.*'

'Sounds like a kind of blancmange,' Darcy said roughly. Wharton ignored him.

'Give another blast at the doorbell, lad. No, they don't do it for gain, these sort of murderers. Generally they suffer so much from pangs of remorse it seems almost a kindness to punish them, take their minds off it, so to speak.'

They waited a little longer, and then Wharton began, 'Well, it doesn't look—' and at that moment the door was opened.

'Mr Hague?' Darcy asked politely. 'We're police officers—'

The haunted, hag-ridden face of the man stared past them unseeingly. His unkempt clothes, blue-stubbled chin, rough hair and gaunt, grey cheeks told of intolerable strain and grief. The wet trowel in his hand spoke of recent activity in the building line.

Wharton, who was tall, could see over the

man's shoulder, and he nudged Darcy and jerked his head suggestively, and Darcy moved a little to one side so that he could see what Wharton could see. What they both saw was, at the other end of the house, down the passage, and through the open door, a shining new expanse of smooth wet concrete covering the kitchen floor. Darcy and Wharton exchanged a glance.

Poor bugger, thought Wharton pityingly. Poor stupid bugger, hasn't even got the sense—comes to the door with a trowel in his hand and the cement still wet. Jesus!

Darcy put a gentle hand on the man's shoulder, and he looked up, tears filling his eyes.

'Can we come in a minute, sir?' Darcy asked quietly. 'We'd like to ask you a few questions.'

*   *   *

It was a funny thing about that concrete. The report of both officers was the same in that both stated quite firmly what they had seen from the door. And yet, as it was discovered later in the investigations into the disappearance and presumed death of Mrs Beatrice Hague, the passage that ran from the front door right through the house performed a double-right-angled bend to accommodate the foot of the stairs. From the front door, you couldn't see the kitchen at all.

We hope you have enjoyed this Large Print book. Other Chivers Press or G.K. Hall Large Print books are available at your library or directly from the publishers. For more information about current and forthcoming titles, please call or write, without obligation, to:

Chivers Press Limited
Windsor Bridge Road
Bath BA2 3AX
England
Tel. (01225) 335336

OR

G.K. Hall
P.O. Box 159
Thorndike, Maine 04986
USA
Tel. (800) 223–2336

All our Large Print titles are designed for easy reading, and all our books are made to last.